FREAK NICK

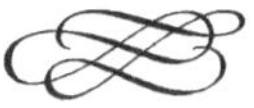

DENISE ESSEX

CONTENTS

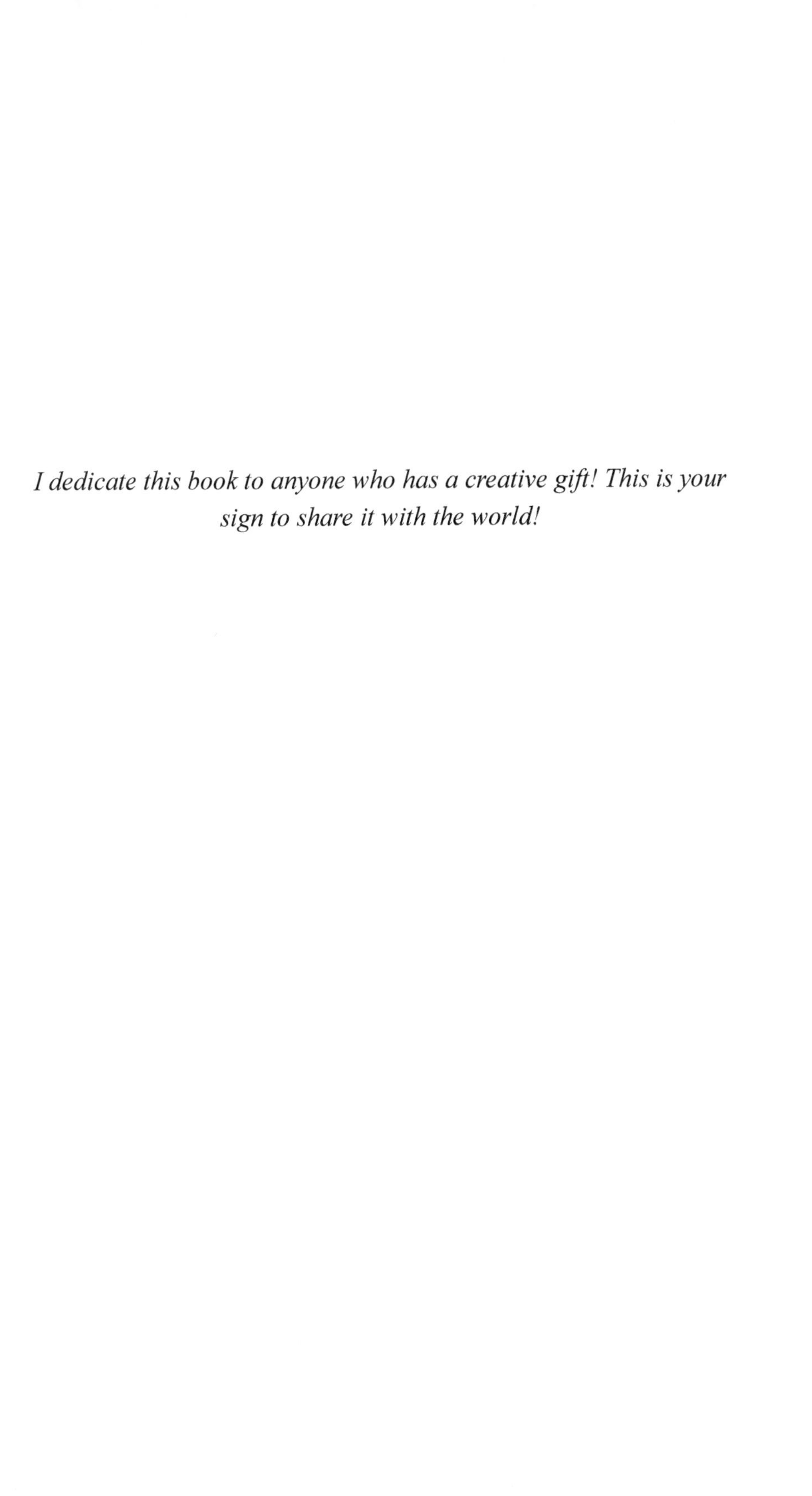

I dedicate this book to anyone who has a creative gift! This is your sign to share it with the world!

ACKNOWLEDGMENTS

I'd like to acknowledge:

My family: *Thank you for allowing me to take up space as an author.*

Marketing Director: *The idea to set a goal to sell 1,000 paperbacks this year was genius!!! Thank you!*

Latisha and proofreaders: *Thank you for your patience and all the invaluable information you share!*

My accountability partners: *Thank you for motivating me with your inspiring goals and holding space for mine!*

Me: *Thank you for continuing to do it, despite your fears. I see you, Goddess!*

Readers: *Thank you for taking time from your life to play in my world and support my art!*

AUTHOR'S NOTE

Dear reader,

Freak Nick is not an erotic romance nor is it an urban fiction title.
*While I include spice in all my books, I am a contemporary romance
author who crafts Sweet Heat reads that are both realistic and
aspirational. Keep an open mind about Nick's story.*

*Please leave a five-star rating and review on Amazon and tag
me on TikTok. Also, be sure to recommend it to your friends. Follow
me on Amazon and sign up for my mailing and SMS list so we can
keep in touch.*

*One of the best ways to support me as an indie author is to
purchase a paperback. Find them on my TikTok for a signed copy,
or Amazon for expedited shipping.*

Mailing list
Get steamy texts from your favorite book baes 💋

With love,
Denise Essex

CHAPTER 1

Kiara

With balls the size of Texas, he lifted her leg from the stool and put her freshly manicured toes in his filthy, intoxicating mouth. I sucked my teeth as the scene unfolded less than a foot away from me and threw back a shot. My bestie, Shay, was on the rebound, and I came out to keep her company until she inevitably found someone new to pass the time. I hadn't intended to be in proximity to Nick "Freak Nick" Young.

Nick's exposed arms were toned. His hard body was on display and contrasted with his almost doll-like facial features. Besides his goatee and thick lips, he was downright beautiful. He was as confusing as a masculine D'Angelo hitting soprano notes when he sang. The woman's eyes rolled to the back of her head as he captured her toes between his lips. He hadn't made a production out of the exchange at all. In fact, the other patrons had no clue what he was up to. *Fuck my life!*

Nick went to the same high school as Shay and me, but he was a few years older. I didn't know him personally, but everyone knew *about* him. His social media account had half a million followers and featured countless reels of him flirting with enticing women, including celebrities like Zanaé. When I was with my son's father, he couldn't stop talking about all the ass Freak Nick got, as if that was a conversation I should ever hear. Darian was toxic. If Nick was anything like my child's father, I wanted nothing to do with him.

Nick took his time peppering her feet with kisses as if it were perfectly normal to suck toes in public. I smacked my lips which earned me a scowl from the beautiful girl who still had her foot in his mouth. His freaky ass had a reputation, but this was the first time I'd gotten a front-row seat.

"Damn, you taste good." His deep baritone boomed in my direction. I was able to hear him perfectly, despite the heavy baseline and the loud chatter between my girl Shay and Mr. Trying Too Damn Hard. I could admit Nick was easy on the eyes, but he was just like the rest of them. *Clearly, all men are whores.*

Why did Shay have to pick this bar? It was twenty minutes from our side of town where people were down to earth and minded their own business. Whenever we crossed over to the north side, the energy shifted. A Nick Young sighting wasn't odd, being that we were in a bougie area. I'd only agreed to come out because Darian had our son for the weekend.

"Asshole," I muttered under my breath as my thoughts shifted to Darian. My son's father was a piece of work. We agreed to have our baby boy by choice. In my young mind, a man wanting to plan a child with me was evidence we'd be good. Darian never mentioned marriage, and I was content because my goal was a family, not a piece of paper. We were on the same page. *Things are so different now.*

"You OK, girl?" Shay asked. She'd leaned down to whisper her concerns.

"I'm going to hit the bathroom. I'll be right back." I stood and straightened the fitted clothing I'd forced myself to squeeze into, kicking my comfy sweats to the side for the evening.

I hadn't made it more than a few steps when Nick bumped into me, spilling his drink down the front of my outfit.

"Shit!" *This can't be happening!* I gasped as the chilly temperature of the liquid seeped into the fabric of my clothes.

"I'm sorry." Nick pulled me toward him with one strong arm and grabbed napkins from the bar with the other. The cedar scent of his cologne wafted into my nose, further pissing me off. His entire demeanor screamed fuck boy. It was as though he'd rehearsed exactly how to dress and act to lure women into his trap.

He gazed down at me appreciatively, like he didn't have this other woman's feet in his mouth. The nerve of this man.

I snatched away from his grasp. "If you weren't so busy with whatever this is, you could watch where you're going." My tone came out harsher than I intended.

"Who is she?" the girl with the toes asked as she inserted herself between Nick and me.

"I accidentally bumped into her, and I'm trying to figure out how to make it right," he hummed. His eyes were locked on me as he placed a sensual kiss on the girl's forehead. "I'm Nick. What was your name, beautiful?"

My nostrils flared. "None of your business."

"Damn, she's rude," the girl with the toes sneered.

The commotion was enough for Shay and her date to walk over.

"What's going on?" my bestie asked.

"This fuck boy spilled liquor on my outfit. I should've stayed home."

"You could get similar treatment if you played your cards right. Maybe if somebody sucked your toes, you wouldn't have such a nasty attitude, because nobody who gets good dick is this wound up," Nick mumbled as he guided his lady away from me.

"What did you say?" After everything Darian put me through, I would not let some inflated ego having overseas ballplayer speak to me in any kind of way. I steadied myself and crossed my arms, furious when they connected with my soaked blouse.

When Nick turned back in my direction, the smirk that covered his face annoyed me, and against my best efforts to deny it, my body responded.

"You heard me." He spoke slowly like he didn't have a care in the world and stroked his facial hair as he continued. "I know your type. You swear you don't need a man for nothing, but you do. It's not a vibrator in the world that could replace me."

I didn't miss the slight puff of his chest, an indicator that he had what it took to back up his claims. Good sex with a fine man who breaks hearts was overrated as hell. No thank you. I was very much satisfied with my flower buddy.

"Let me pay for your outfit. Your mean ass is pretty as hell," he added smugly.

There was silence between our small crowd as everyone awaited my comeback. Nick didn't break his gaze, no matter how much the girl beside him huffed. As I stormed off in the direction of the bathroom, heat covered my cheeks.

Shay told her date she would call him later and was on my heels in no time. Once we were inside the bathroom, the lights grew in intensity, giving me a headache. The floor-length mirror propped up against the corner of the wall reflected the mess Nick made.

"Girl, what was that about? Nick Young is fine as hell."

Shay couldn't hold a thought to save her life. I hated the way people threw around labels as though they were certified psychiatrists, but I was sure my girl had ADHD. I would ignore the part about Nick being fine, because that had nothing to do with our debate. I was pissed because he acted like he walked on water.

"I hate men. I swear I do."

"Don't say that, Keke." She said it in the tone she used

whenever I was tripping. Maybe I was. "Admit he was fine, though. I haven't been close to him in years. I think he got finer."

I mean mugged her until we both burst into uncontrollable giggles. I could admit Nick was fine, but his genetic blessings didn't give him a license to discuss my sex life or to call me bitter. He had some nerves.

Nick

Sierra was impressed by my social media presence. She wasn't the first, and she wouldn't be the last. I'd barely touched down in Saint Des when she slid in my DMs asking to link. There was nothing sexier than a woman with a fresh pedicure and the energy she gave, which was why I ended up with her pretty toes in my mouth.

We'd messaged a total of two days online, and here we were. I didn't subscribe to moving too fast or two slow. If the connection was there, that shit didn't matter. If it wasn't, what was the rush? Most of those time constraints came from worrying about what someone else thought. Sierra had already gotten that other pretty chick's panties in a bunch, because her mean ass secretly wanted the same attention.

I hadn't been home in far too long. The transition was smooth, and the club had a stress-free vibe. Now that I didn't have Sierra's feet in my mouth, we were in an easy conversation, although she was much more attractive with her mouth closed. Women as fine as her struggled in the personality department, which didn't come as a surprise to me. As long as she didn't ask me how I got my name, we would be good.

"Freak Nick," she purred. I'd bought Sierra two drinks, and she was already acting drunk. My body tensed. If she wanted to fuck, she didn't have to pretend it was the alcohol talking. That got old once we were out of our early twenties.

"How'd you get your name?"

There went my buzz. I high-key hated that name. I was thirty damn years old. Going by the name Freak Nick made me like one of those dudes who kept hanging around the high school after they graduated. At some point, it was time to hang it up. I hadn't changed my social media handle because I didn't take anything online seriously. Freak Nick was my representative. A dated one at that.

"It's super overblown. More of an online thing, you know?"

Her hand rested on my thigh. "Afraid you can't live up to the hype?"

I counted to ten in my head. She couldn't know in the past decade I had this conversation as many times as basketball players were asked how tall they were. That shit was annoying, too, but I learned to accept I was with me my whole life. These other people weren't used to my name or my height.

"You familiar with line names?" I asked as she peered up at me with doe eyes.

"From your fraternity? Your line name was Freak Nick?"

I nodded. "And before you ask, I don't know how much of a 'freak' I am." I used air quotes when I said freak. "I just love pussy and the women it's attached to, and I don't bother trying to hide it like some men do. One of the best things God did was make a woman. I love the way you smell and taste. I honestly can't get enough."

"Oh, you're that kind of freak. So, no tossing me around and bending my legs behind my ears?"

"I never said I couldn't if that's what you're into. But also," I added, as I swept her hair behind her ear. She'd done it about a hundred times, and I found the habit quite arousing.

She sucked in a breath as her eyes closed briefly.

"There's nothing basic about missionary with the right amount of chemistry. It's not a requirement to get into every Kamasutra position unless it happens organically."

"I think I'll call you Sexy Nick." She wet her lips. "Or Charming Nick. It suits you."

"Whatever you like, sweetheart."

"I wanna see for myself."

My eyebrows flew up. "Are you ready to go right now? We just got here," I offered with a chuckle.

"I'm feeling you, and I never said we had to leave."

Her annoying questions about how similar I was to my social media persona had flown out of the window, and my dick had fully awakened. Her eyes fell between my legs, and when they returned to my face, they were full of raging lust.

I stood and gently grabbed her elbow.

"Where are we going?" she asked.

"I'm about to let you see for yourself."

I'd been to this club a dozen times because the owner was a good friend of my fraternity brother, Cyrus. Cyrus lived about an hour away but had an uncle living in Saint Des. There was a private room in the back. All I had to do was text him for the code. I sent the message once I'd led Sierra to a dark corner to sit until he hit me back.

I pulled her on my lap and immediately let my hands have their way. She had zero complaints. I reached my hand in front of us and pushed her panties to the side beneath the flimsy dress she wore.

"Damn, you ready like this?"

She nodded, and the vibration of her moan reverberated down to my lap. I slid my finger inside of her and felt the grip surrounding it. No wonder she was ready. It had been quite some time since she'd shared her cheeks with anyone. I swept her hair out of my way and ran my tongue across the back of her neck. She rocked in my lap, creating friction between us. Sierra leaned into my chest, begging me to take her right there. Although I didn't have a problem fucking in front of people, I wasn't convinced *she* could handle the exposure.

Her mouth found my ear. I fumbled with my phone after it buzzed with a reply from the owner—the room was ready for me. He said he owed Cyrus a favor, and it was no sweat for me to use it for as long as I liked. Sierra saw the message. Her lids lowered and her mouth formed an O.

"You sure you wanna see?" I asked with a smirk on my face. I didn't consider myself any freakier than the next man. I loved fucking. I didn't have to have every woman who looked my way, but a fine one like Sierra couldn't help but see first-hand why I'd earned the name. If that made me a freak, so be it.

I navigated to the private room, holding Sierra in front of me while we walked. I wanted her to feel how hard she had me. I closed and locked the door and immediately pulled her dress up. I dropped to my knees and took an audible breath in.

"Damn, you smell good."

She angled her head to look, but I was in no hurry to move along. Maybe it was a little freaky, but I wanted to have a silent conversation with her pussy. Sierra opened her mouth, but I held up my hand.

"What?" she asked with her perfectly manicured eyebrow lifted.

"Your pussy is talking to me."

Sierra laughed. The flirtatious sound tickled my ears. "What is she saying?"

"She said it's been a long time, which is why you're acting all flustered and in a hurry."

I stroked between her legs while she had a fight with her own damn pussy.

"Tell her to shut up because we both need this."

I pulled a condom from my pocket with my free hand, while I kept my eyes locked on hers.

I increased the pace and pressure of my hand between Sierra's thighs. Her legs shook as she threw her head back. She had an orgasm before I could even get inside of her. I spun her around and sprinkled kisses across the thin fabric covering her ass. I pulled them down to her ankles and watched as she stepped out of red panties.

As soon as the condom was safely in place, I pushed on her back until she bent forward. I gripped her hips.

"Y'all ready for me?" I groaned. Her pleasure was my priority, but somehow, pleasing a woman always got me riled up in the process. I wanted to tease her, only the teasing was bringing me close to my own limit.

"Please," she begged.

I still hadn't moved.

She angled her head back to see me. "I said please," she fussed.

"I was waiting for your pussy to respond."

I threw her a wink then pushed inside of her tight oasis. "Got damn!"

Kiara

As much as I needed a break from my baby boy, Kace, I missed him terribly when he was gone. Sundays were supposed to be Darian's, but whenever Kace stayed with him, he never got enough sleep to prepare for the coming school day. We agreed he'd bring him back home by six, yet it was already eight thirty p.m.

I scrolled my phone, pausing when a picture of Nick and the girl from the bar showed up on my timeline. I could admit she was pretty. Her rich chocolate skin was blemish free, and her auburn-colored eyes bore into me through the screen. Before I was tempted to fall down a rabbit hole, the rattling of Darian's speakers notified the block of his presence.

"One, two, three. I coparent with ease. Four, five, six, my son deserves this. Seven, eight, nine, I'm too pretty to do time," I said with a giggle. "Ten, I release unrealistic expectations and when I get pissed off, I'll start at one and begin again."

For ten years, I chanted that affirmation. While it kept my nervous system regulated and my hands off Darian, it was powerless to keep my attitude toward my son's father in check. *Why the hell would he bring Kace home this late? It's like he couldn't care less about our child's need to transition.*

Kace bumbled through the door with his hands full and a charming smile on his face.

"Sorry I'm late, Mama," Kace blurted, as if he could control the time he arrived.

"It's not your fault, son," I assured him as I pulled him in for a hug.

"Yes, it is. I told his ass he had to clean up before we left. He waited 'til the last minute."

I was all for Kace having chores, but Darian's idea of cleaning up meant his entire apartment was in better condition than when

Kace got there. My father was a hard ass when it came to discipline, and my stepbrothers got it much worse than me. I also couldn't teach Kace to be a man any more than Darian could teach me how to be a mother, yet I found myself biting the inside of my lip often. I wished Darian would be realistic. Did he have to do the things he expected our eleven-year-old child to do? I was 90 percent sure he didn't.

Kace ambled toward his bedroom as Darian's eyes raked over my body. I repeated the coparenting mantra in my head and prayed my true desire to choke this man didn't bubble up and out of me.

"I'm worried about Kace."

"What now, Kiara? He's fine. A little extra cleaning won't hurt him. It will prepare him for the world. He needs to know life is not all hugs and kisses from his mommy."

"I'm always going to hug my baby, but that's beside the point. He's changing. And I don't mean the part about him growing up. I fully expect him to become a young man. It's his anger. I tell him to pick up his clothes, and he puffs his chest out. One time, he even threw something."

"Towns," Darian barked, referring to our son by my last name. I still couldn't figure out if he used it because he was bitter I hadn't given Kace his last name, or if he wanted to remind our son who the Alpha was. Dealing with my child's father was downright exhausting. *At least Kace knows his dad. Just because Darian's an ass and things didn't work out between us doesn't mean I'm not lucky to have him in Kace's life.*

"Sir," Kace bellowed as he bopped back into the room. It was harder and harder to recognize my baby boy now that his locs had grown and there was already a faint line above his upper lip. His birthday was earlier this month, but wasn't eleven too young for all these changes? He'd been a preteen for two seconds. Kace's anger had gotten to where I feared he'd lose control, which was why I wanted to have a conversation with Darian *about* Kace, not with Kace.

Darian walked into our son's space, and my heart dropped.

"You throwing things at your mother's house?"

"Uh," Kace muttered as his eyes jumped from mine up to his father's, who towered menacingly over him. "Yes, sir."

Before I could take my next breath, my son was snatched up by his shirt with his feet barely on the ground.

"The hell is your problem, boy?"

"Darian, please."

He let go, but the interaction was totally uncalled for.

"Go to your room while I talk to your father," I said quickly before things got out of hand.

"What do you want me to do? Boys don't respond to words. They only understand actions, and if he's getting to the point where you can't control him, he needs to stay with me full time."

My stomach fell to my feet. I figured there might come a time to discuss Kace moving in with his dad, but I assumed it would be after he became a teenager.

I sat in the nearest chair and let out a defeated breath. "It's too soon. He's only eleven."

"You can't keep babying him then complain he isn't listening to you."

"You're right."

Darian dramatically turned around in a full circle. "I'm what?" His dark eyebrows—identical to my son's—lifted to the heavens.

He rubbed his hands together and gave me a look that used to put me in the mood. These days, it did nothing more than make my skin crawl.

"I can always come back and stick around here full time."

"Don't you live with a girl you're currently cheating on?" I stood and crossed my arms, annoyed he'd gone from a somewhat concerned father to a creeper in a matter of moments. Darian broke my heart and was the reason I hated men. We'd made a child in love, and after Kace was born, all hell broke loose. I walked to the door and opened it wordlessly.

"Remember what I said about Kace. If he needs more discipline, I got you."

If I could trust you not to take things too far, I wouldn't hesitate to let him stay with you. If you could discipline him in an age-appropriate manner, I'd put my emotions about missing him aside and do what's best for him, but you're too inconsistent and too damn unpredictable for me to leave my child in your care more than what I already do.

"Sure thing." I gave him a polite nod and closed the door.

Dinner was already made. I'd enjoy a meal with Kace and have him in bed at a somewhat decent hour for school. The last thing I needed was any reports from his teachers about the anger I saw at home.

Nick

Saint Des was a warm hug of familiarity I didn't know I needed. The Darkhaven Mavericks had gotten some of my best years and hands down my best ball playing highlights to date. I had no regrets about not re-signing my contract. My mind was made up going into the international league that I would leave on my own terms before any scandals or any career ending injuries if I had anything to do with it.

No competitive athlete in their right mind would admit they weren't at optimal capacity, but I could because being a ballplayer wasn't my entire identity. I'd slowed down a bit. I didn't have the intensity I needed to perform at my best. It was time to hang up my sneakers.

My baby sister, Jackie, had been calling me for the last few weeks. I despised talking on the phone. I did it because women liked it. I preferred to see my family in person. I wanted to look her and my niece and nephew in the eyes to make sure they were good. Too much could get lost in translation. I felt people's energy and audio calls were a buffer between me and my day ones.

She was likely pissed by now because I tried not to go more than three weeks without either video calling or flying them out to see me. I was home for good, and I would make up for lost time. Jackie would probably kick my ass, but the lumps would be worth it. My introspection was interrupted by the familiar tone of my fraternity brother Cyrus's ringtone.

"Whooooa yeah!" he yelled into the phone.

"Yeah, yeah, crewwwww!" I yelled back, scaring my driver half to death. "Sorry," I whispered, trying but failing to hide my chuckle. My car wouldn't arrive for another week. Until then, I'd survive on rideshares.

"You back in Timbuktu?" Cyrus teased.

"I guess you could call Saint Des a spiritual mecca of sorts, but yeah, I'm back. I just touched down."

"Cool. When can I slide through?"

"Damn. You trying to see me already? Or some chicks?"

"It's an untapped market is all I'm saying, and I know you know exactly where to find them, Freak Nick." His voice was delicate and high-pitched when he said my line name.

It was Cyrus who spilled my history to the other Nu Omega Tau brothers. On one hand, I did have an overblown reputation with women. I unapologetically loved the opposite sex out loud. There were few things I enjoyed more than being with and inside a woman. Everything before and after getting ass was equally satisfying. I didn't have to try hard either. Some of my boys judged me for showing interest in women the way I did; they said it made me look thirsty.

Thirsty or not, word got around campus that I was willing to go to almost any length with the women I spent time with. Men were competitive, but no one was more comparative than a woman. It was as though they needed to see what the hype was for themselves. And it was a hype. All I'd done was lick a few toes and fuck at a party, and suddenly, I was labeled a freaky man. It was mind boggling that was all it took to be placed on a pedestal.

I could admit I had a thing for feet. A woman with well-kept toes was a turn on. As far as the college party, I hadn't done anything spectacular.

There was a girl who gave me energy every time we were together, but we could never get on the same page as far as linking up. She was in a sorority, and she had a difficult major. While students whispered about how nasty I could be, she was labeled a good girl. That night, she let loose and pulled me into a room. I was willing to wait to hook up and assumed she wanted more privacy than the closed door of an after-party, but there was no way in hell I would turn her down.

At some point during the party sex, we were interrupted. Somebody thought it would be funny to burst open the doors while I was knee deep in her cheeks. They got the shock of their lives when I didn't pull out on their account. I asked if she wanted me to stop and when she shook her head no and moaned 'please don't stop,' I kept going.

With an audience of a dozen or more peers, I knocked the brakes off her pussy, changing positions like I didn't have a care in the world. The fact that guys and girls alike watched turned us both on and only fueled my reputation as a freak.

Getting women was ingrained in my DNA though. Since as far back as I could remember, my dad told me he swiped my mom away from her steady boyfriend at the infamous Freaknik.

I had no idea what any of it meant at the time, but as I got older, I learned Pops had serious swag to get the attention of my mother in that environment. She was forced into going by, in her words, one of her fast-in-the-ass cousins. She insisted everyone acted as though they had no sense and no home training. When my father approached her, she immediately waved him off. But Pops was determined to get with my mom. He didn't let up because he'd convinced himself my mom was his future baby mama. By the end of the weekend, he'd worn her down, and the rest was history.

I told Cyrus the story to vouch for the fact that pimping was in my blood. I never in a million years thought that he'd use the information when I was on line with the other Nu Omega Tau pledges. It had to have been one of the most epic line names ever. To this day, everyone referred to me as "Freak Nick."

"I do. Are you trying to slide through tonight?"

"I can," he said with way too much excitement in his voice. "My uncle's been on my ass about making my way there. He's been pushing me to take over his gym, but I ain't got the patience for a bunch of old church ladies pretending to work out."

"Your ass needs to slow down. That's why Uncle Mitch is on your head. You on baby number six?" I teased.

"I got two kids, and you know it. Running a gym is like saying I'm never playing ball again."

"I'm sick of training and I played basketball longer than you. We ain't never going back to them days. It's time to do something else," I pressed. I needed to hear those words as much as he did.

Cyrus fell quiet.

"Let me have at least one night with the fam before I start ripping and running as Mama Young would say." I chuckled at the endearment my friends used for my mom. She was loved and respected. Mrs. Young was far too impersonal for her, so Mama Young it was.

"Alright, bet, but tomorrow, we're going out, and you're showing me around Saint Des. I'm trying to meet my future baby mama."

"I'm telling my pops you using all his moves." The fact that Cyrus was still so deeply familiar with my parents' origin story was probably the reason my line name stuck.

"You think I'm worried when I'm not." He kissed his teeth, and as if he'd already moved the phone from his face, his voice was faint when he said, "Later."

"Yup."

I was only slightly ashamed I'd stayed in a hotel for the first week I was back in town. I wouldn't disrespect my folks coming in and out with the hours I kept. The car pulled up to my parents' home, and that hug feeling intensified. I understood why some kids never moved out. The relief and safety of being near people who loved me most was unmatched.

"Is that my baby?" my mom crooned from the front yard. She was always out there trimming and grooming.

I gave a nod to the driver and dropped my bags. My mom was tiny, even though her heart was enormous. She jogged in my direction, and I easily lifted her so she could see my face up close.

"Boy, put me down. Did you get taller?"

"I think you got smaller, Ma," I teased. At five feet, six inches, my mom never felt short unless she was around my dad, Jackie, and me. To us, she was a runt, and we never let her forget it. When I released her, she hung on with her arms wrapped under my ribs like she hadn't seen me in years.

"I was here for Christmas."

"I know. It's your sister," she started.

"Uncle Nick!" my niece, Elle, screamed from the porch.

"Jellybean. Is that you?" I returned, releasing my mom to get to my favorite and only niece.

She jumped from the porch, fully confident I would catch her. I loved this girl like she was my own, and it was insane how much I missed her. I downplayed how long it had been with my mom but quickly changed my tune when my eight-year-old nephew, Eli, stepped onto the porch much taller than he'd been six short months ago.

"What's up, Uncle Nick?" he said nonchalantly. With my free arm, I pulled my nephew in and tossed him up.

"Nick, don't come in here riling these kids up. I just got them settled."

"Where's Jackie?" I asked. The vibe was off. My mom wasn't in grandma mode at all. She made a point to remind Jackie her only job was to love her grandkids then return them back to their mother.

"She's inside, but Gram said we need to let her sleep," Eli added.

My head swung in my mom's direction. She'd returned to her lawn care, and an eerie feeling settled over me. Jackie and I were close, and although I hadn't spoken to her in almost a month, I hoped I hadn't missed anything major.

I patted Eli's head and pinched Elle's still chunky cheeks before gathering my bags and stepping inside. Jackie was curled up in the guest bedroom like she'd been staying here.

I snatched the blankets off. "Where am I supposed to stay? You in here funking up the blankets."

Jackie lifted weakly, and I immediately felt like shit.

"You good? What's wrong, Jack?"

"Hey, big bro," she said with a faint smile on her beautiful face. If this was someone's first time seeing the two of us, they'd swear she was the oldest. Life had gotten my baby sister down.

"I messed up for real this time."

I took a seat on the chair across from her and gave her my full attention.

"Look at you. Always so handsome. Did you have to beat the girls off at the airport with a stick?" she teased.

I smirked because she wasn't wrong. Black women swore gray sweatpants were some type of lingerie. I'd only worn them because of my flight. It was the beginning of summer, so I'd spend most of my time in basketball shorts.

"Stop changing the subject."

"Whose number did you get? I gotta make sure I don't know her."

"Some chick named Sierra. But I don't wanna talk about girls right now. What's going on, Jack? You're scaring me." I moved and took a seat beside her on the bed, cringing because I knew better than to sit there with my outside clothes on.

"I got caught holding something. I went to court and the judge won't fine me or make me do any time, but I have to check myself into rehab for at least thirty days."

"What?"

"I'm scared, Nicky." She hadn't called me that since we were kids. Truth be told, I was terrified now.

"I thought you were done with all that," I said in the most non accusatory tone I could conjure.

"I was until… I wasn't. I don't want to leave the kids for a month."

"If it's as bad as it sounds, you have to."

"They won't understand—"

"Trust me, you'd rather do a few weeks apart to handle whatever has you back on that shit than for them to see you messed up."

"Eli saw me once," she said with tears in her eyes. "He thought I was being silly, but when he gets older, he'll put two and two together. He also knows something is going on, and I don't know how to explain to him I'm leaving. I might be able to call, but it won't be a good idea for them to visit me while I'm there."

My shoulders sagged. "How can I help?"

She leaned over and rested her head on my shoulder. "You already are."

"I'm serious."

"Me too. You're newly back in town, and the last thing you need is to worry about me and my drama."

"Jackie Lynn Young, do you need me to take the kids over the weekends or something?"

"Mama and Daddy can't keep up with the kids, so maybe for the month?" she asked barely above a whisper.

I created space between us to look into her eyes. My baby sister had the weight of the world on her shoulders. It was beyond my capacity to understand how we had the same parents and grew up in the same household, yet she'd fallen victim to drug addiction. "OK."

"Nick?" Her eyes doubled in size. Maybe she hadn't meant to admit how much help she needed, and while I might have been in over my head, I would do whatever it took to help her get back on her feet.

"Jack?" I said, mocking her in the sassy tone she always used with me.

I stood.

"Where are you going?"

"I'm letting you sleep, and then I'm looking for apartments."

"Are you sure about this?"

"Once I tell them kids, you'll have a hell of a time untelling them," I teased then tossed a pillow at her.

"Thank you, Nick."

"Of course."

CHAPTER 2

Nick

This was Eli and Elle's second week at Rube Foster Charter School. Jackie started rehab shortly after I returned, which only gave me enough time to arrange a place to rent until I could secure more long-term housing. I would have paid for the kids to go to the private school with the highest ratings but was scolded by my mom who insisted my niece and nephew needed a well-rounded experience where the staff reflected the student body.

She was right. I'd prepared myself for my niece and nephew to fight me about all the recent changes in their life, but it never happened. The moment I laid eyes on my baby sister, it was clear she would need the full thirty days of her mandatory rehab stay ordered by the judge.

My sister was caught boosting. She'd picked up a gang of horrible habits at the private school we attended growing up. Jackie got good grades. She appeared to be the golden child, while I was always pushing the boundaries set for me by any authority figure. I discovered her usage one weekend when our parents were out of town. She assured me it wasn't a big deal, but even as a teenager, I was certain nobody used recreationally while they were alone. Jackie ignored me when I told her those girls would bring her down.

I hadn't been able to protect her from the ugliness of our world, but I could damn sure help her now that Elle and Eli were displaced. Part of me wanted to be selfish and take time to reintegrate into life without ball before I agreed to another commitment like being a full-time caregiver, but the urge left me as quickly as it came. I loved those kids like they were mine from day zero. I pestered Jackie into sending me every sonogram although I had no earthly idea what any of the blobs were. In my heart, they were my future niece and nephew.

Other than a hiccup with my barely furnished apartment, Eli and Elle fit into my world seamlessly, and they were both thrilled about the new school. I had my eyes on the teachers, but so far, they hadn't given me any red flags. I was officially on full-time uncle-daddy duty, and there was no way any foul shit would go down on my watch.

My biggest complaint was all the homework *I* was assigned. My nephew was quite self-sufficient, but there was no way they expected my five-year-old niece to complete these tasks. The drop-off line was a waste of time and gas. I routinely pretended not to understand the rules, bypassing it completely by parking and walking Eli and Elle to the door. The female security guard had a crush and waved me on. She hardly put up a fight the first time I walked up with my crew in tow.

"I can't get a hug?" I boomed. Eli had advised me not to do this in public, but I couldn't help myself.

Elle jumped into my arms. She wiggled out when she saw another girl from her class. I had to chase Eli down because he'd gotten fast. I bear hugged him from the back and released him when a disrespectful voice pierced my ears.

"Why you out here looking like a slouch with my seed in your care?" someone yelled.

He was short and needed his bark to be louder than his childish body. It was obvious by his harsh tone that he didn't know how to speak to a woman. And if I'd heard him right, this was his baby mama. I released an irritated breath. My sister didn't have help from her baby's daddy which was why if my parents couldn't step up, I was the only other viable option. No matter how well Jackie treated that fool, he disregarded her, and she deserved better.

Keep walking. This ain't got nothing to do with you.

I was on my way until a feminine voice I recognized floated into my ears.

"Darian, please don't make a scene. Why are you here?"

It was the mean ass girl from the bar. She had a hell of a lot more attitude with me when I accidentally spilled a drink on her. How could a woman that fine be this watered down when it mattered? He was the one who had earned her wrath, not me. I had something that could straighten them both out.

"They called me saying they wanted to meet with his parents. I'm his parent, Kiara," buddy screeched.

She had her back to me, and I'd almost forgotten why I'd stopped. Kiara had to have been a track star with the toned legs and extraordinary ass to match. Other than her foul mouth, she was someone I'd consider adding to the roster. Her fitted pants left little to the imagination. Was she on her way to the gym?

"We had the meeting before school so he could still make it to class on time. Darian, can we please talk about this later?"

Kiara's head was on a swivel. Although he didn't give a damn, she didn't want to embarrass herself any further in front of her kid's school.

"That's your problem. If you spent more time worrying about Kace instead of trying to get back with ya boy, we wouldn't be in this situation. 'Can we talk later' is code for you asking to come over. We both know how those conversations always end."

Her shoulders sank. Was this man for real? It was obvious who the prize of the relationship was. His little man syndrome had him abusing this beauty to make himself bigger. Against my better judgment, my sneakers made a B-line in the direction of that small waist above a mountain of ass. *Damn!*

I draped my arm around her and pulled her close, then I whispered loud enough for him to hear. "Hey, baby. I thought that was you."

She attempted to yank away from me, but I kept her in place, giving her a knowing look. I cleared my throat and bounced my eyes between her and her baby daddy who had his chest puffed out and his brows furrowed as I suspected he would.

"Who the hell are you supposed to be?" Darian asked.

"Kiara didn't tell you?" I bent down further and placed my lips on her neck, causing her to shudder. She huffed, but her body couldn't lie. *Is she acting for him, or is she enjoying me for real?*

I returned my eyes to the much smaller man with the Napoleon complex and offered my hand. "I'm Nick. Kiara's man."

She tried to slip away again, and this time, I let her so I could slap her ass. The yelp that escaped her lips made it worth it, despite the scowl on her sassy ass face.

"Wait a damn minute. Freak Nick?" His voice had risen several octaves once recognition clouded his features.

"The one and only," I returned.

Darian's jaw was clenched, and his fists were balled. He opened his mouth to speak but was interrupted by the security guard.

"Everything OK?" she asked as her eyes raked over me.

"Yes, ma'am. Kiara and I were on our way to the gym," I said, winking at the guard and throwing a nod at Darian.

We hadn't made it more than a foot away from the scene when she whisper-yelled, "What the fuck are you doing?"

I gazed down at her and gave her my biggest smile. "Pissing off your man."

She peeked behind her to find Darian watching as we headed toward my car.

"That's not my man. He hasn't held the title in years. And where are you taking me? My car is the other way," she fussed.

"Damn, baby. What would it look like if I let you leave in your own car?"

"It would look like I drove myself here to drop off my son, and I'm leaving the same way I came. How did you even know I was here? Are you stalking me?"

I opened my passenger door and waited for her to get in. After another backward glance in Darian's direction, she relented and relaxed those miraculous cheeks in my ride. Pure satisfaction surrounded me. I got her mean ass riled while also pissing off her man in one fell swoop.

I peeked over when the screen of her phone lit up, in time to see a message from her baby daddy.

KACE'S DAD:

I don't know how you tricked him, but I
know for a fact y'all ain't fuckin'

She wasted no time firing off her response.

KIARA:

That's your problem, you think you know
everything

KACE'S DAD:

There's no way you wouldn't have rubbed
this in my face the moment you had a
man. Are you paying him to make me
jealous?

She heaved a breath and turned her phone upside down. Kiara had doubled down on the fact that we were kicking it. I wanted to get her man pissed off, but she'd confirmed we were an item. How long did she plan to keep this up? And how far was she willing to go to piss him off?

"Now what?" she asked with her arms crossed.

My attention fell to the area where her arms now resided, still intrigued although she couldn't have been more than a B cup.

"I take you to the gym or to breakfast. I'm good with whichever."

She didn't have to stay in my car, and she certainly didn't have to let me take her anywhere, but I wouldn't be me if I didn't push the envelope. I reached my arm across her—prepared to have her slap it away—and buckled her seat belt, watching her the entire time.

"Safety first."

Her long lashes fluttered upward, but it only fueled my pursuit of whatever this was. I had my car in gear when Sierra pulled her custom whip beside me. She caught me by surprise—because where the fuck did she come from—but I was quick to play it off. I hadn't done anything wrong, and the last time I checked, I was a free agent.

"Damn, you look good," I said, feeling the need to state the obvious. Sierra never had an off day. I'd linked with her twice since the club. I had reservations about how well I'd adjust to Saint Des, but my first night out, I met up with Sierra. She was a big city girl stuck in a small town. While it was initially a relief to spend time with someone who was comfortable with fine dining—and other experiences people from my hometown weren't—I prayed it wouldn't become a problem. I was big city but small town in my heart.

She had stars in her eyes like I was a brand-new pair of sparkly shoes until her eyes collided with my passenger princess.

"Who are you?"

Kiara straightened her back like she was a millisecond from snapping on Sierra.

"The next chick to have my toes in Nick's mouth, that's who," she quipped, barely shifting her eyes in Sierra's direction.

Damn! I was starting to like Kiara's attitude. It was attractive as hell. I enjoyed getting her riled up because she was cuter when she was pissed, but she was about to blow my entanglement. Sierra was fine fine. She was what I categorized as a sure thing. I didn't have a ton of free time, but when the kids were with my parents, I could call her, and she'd come without hesitation. Now she was face-to-face with the reality of the reputation I'd worked hard to downplay since I'd been back in Saint Des.

People assumed because of my nickname, I entertained different women every day of the week, but it was far from the truth. It was exhausting explaining I was only a freak with the woman I was with. I didn't like a big roster, quiet as it was kept. Two or three was my max. Anything beyond that was complicated—and I did not do complicated.

My freakish ways weren't for any beautiful woman I saw. It was about me being comfortable in my skin and uninhibited with someone I invited into my space. I was a freak, not a whore, but now Sierra's top lip was damn near lifted to her nose like I was full of shit.

"Oh, that's your MO? You put any raggedy bitch's feet in your mouth, Nick?"

Kiara giggled beside me.

I turned my head to find her unbothered face in her phone.

"She called herself raggedy."

I scratched my head as Kiara sighed like she'd just laughed at the funniest shit ever.

"Can we go before she gets any louder?" she asked, shifting in my passenger seat.

"Sierra, I'm gonna call you," I tried. But she threw up her middle finger and peeled out unnecessarily since we were near an elementary school.

I drove Kiara and myself in the direction of a diner I loved. It was low-key, and while most of the women I dealt with stuck their noses up at the greasy eatery, Kiara didn't seem bothered. Her fingers typed furiously on her phone. She was probably talking shit about me, but she hadn't demanded I take her back to her car, so I wasn't complaining.

"You hungry?" I asked as I opened her door. "I would have taken you for a workout, but I already ran, and I'm hungry as shit."

She shrugged her shoulders. "I have classes most afternoons to keep me in shape. I could eat."

My mind reeled at the type of classes she had lined up. In my perfect world, she taught strip tease classes to sexy, desperate housewives, which would make her a former stripper and me the luckiest man ever to accidentally hit the jackpot.

"Have you ever been here?" I asked as I held the door open for her.

"I've driven by it, but it doesn't look like the safest spot for me. It's giving heavy truck stop vibes."

"You say that now; wait 'til you taste the food. And most of the people who eat here are harmless."

Her arms were crossed when we stepped inside, and they stayed that way until we were seated.

"Nick Young, welcome back, my boy," Dale said. If your eyes were closed, you'd swear he was mixed with something.

Dale was one of those non-melanated men who grew up around nothing but black people. He didn't try on the culture like it was a costume—it was literally all he knew. Naturally, he married a black woman and had some kids. Dale went above and beyond to make sure they had what they needed, including working overtime at the diner until he made a profit. He was featured on a best diners list in a national magazine.

Dale went from a local white dude who everyone was surprised could cook to officially on the map with folks from the north side and beyond the city limits frequenting his south side establishment.

"And who do we have here?" Dale asked.

Kiara blushed at the attention, even though she fought tooth and nail to keep up the attitude she'd worn since I swooped her from the school.

"Nick, tell me you ain't on a day date." He whipped out his phone dramatically and checked the screen. "April sixteenth. Let me mark this day in my calendar, because in all the years I've known you, I ain't never seen you with a woman you ain't related to outside of a club or the mall."

Kiara laughed. Her smile was almost distracting enough for me to forget Dale's insult.

"Take your clear ass out of here with all that," I tried. It wasn't intentional for me to be out with Kiara. I was pretending to be her man and got caught up in the moment. As mean as she'd been to me, there was no way we'd go any further than today and maybe an occasional performance at the school. I was intrigued, nonetheless.

"That's all you got? You know the sistas like vanilla when y'all don't treat them like the queens they are," he said, earning him a smirk from Kiara.

"Can you leave us alone until we decide what we want? Where's your waitress?" I asked with a chuckle of my own. He wasn't wrong about how black women were treated, and his wife didn't play those types of games.

"I sure can," Dale said while throwing a wink in Kiara's

direction. "Maybe I'll let Stacy off the hook and wait on you myself," he said as he left us with two brunch menus.

Kiara peered around the place with apprehension etched across her beautiful features. There wasn't much in Dale's Diner in the aesthetics department, but what he lacked in decor, he more than made up for with rich, fulfilling food that made you want to slap anybody.

"Trust me. The food is not a reflection of the interior design," I said once we were alone.

"You don't act like this on social media."

"Who said?"

"I mean, where the hos at?" She lifted her menu, turned her head to peek behind us dramatically, then bent her body to look under the table where our booth was located.

"You got jokes?"

Her smile returned, showcasing a small space between her teeth. It was so slight I hadn't seen it until now.

"I'm being sincere. I've seen your social media, and your reputation precedes you. Where the hos at?"

"My life is a little different these days."

"Oh, right. You have practically grown kids you've decided to help raise since you're done with basketball."

"The fuck?" I didn't try to hide the irritation in my voice. Was this chick for real? "Wow. When I said you had an attitude problem at the bar, what I meant to say was you're bitter. You don't know me."

I leaned forward, ready to say fuck her meal.

She rolled her eyes and did a little shrug that made me want to physically dominate her until she learned some respect, but she wouldn't be worth the hassle.

"I saw you with two beautiful children less than an hour ago, and unless you're one of those overprotective dads, I've never seen you post or even mention them before today."

I stood and dropped a handful of twenties. "You want to stay, or you want a ride?"

Her eyes widened.

"Either way, I'm out. I lost my appetite." I wouldn't put my hands on a woman, but she had me at the edge of my limit. I wouldn't sit here and justify my niece and nephew to her. I didn't owe her shit.

"I'll stay. I'm sure Dale will take good care of me. He could take me back to my car after," Kiara stated with sarcasm dripping from each of her taunting words. She shared her smile again, but this time, it didn't reach her eyes.

I leaned down and whispered beside her ear. "If I'm a deadbeat daddy, you're a homewrecker. Dale is married with kids of his own. Good luck with that." I pulled back far enough to lock eyes with her, sharing a devious smile of my own. *Bitter bitch.*

Kiara

Nick was right about the food and about Dale. While I ate my meal alone, his beautiful wife floated into the restaurant, standing out like a sore thumb. Her wardrobe and demeanor didn't fit. She was a kept woman who oozed low-key wealth. Their initial embrace made me look away, although they weren't overtly sexual.

There was genuine love between them, and it kind of pissed me off. Freak Nick had the nerve to call me a sidepiece. He'd pulled a UNO reverse card that knocked the wind out of me. I wasn't into white men. Nick wouldn't need to be defensive if he hadn't gotten triggered by my comment about his children.

Why can't men do right by their families? And how did sis get lucky with Dale? It's like Dale and my daddy are the only decent men in Saint Des.

Even my dad couldn't get it together when it came to women.

The rideshare took me back to the school, and I prayed I wouldn't run into anyone. I had several hours before I needed to pick up Kace. It left me with enough time to prepare for my afternoon classes. Nothing calmed me like choreographing a dance class for young people. The drive from Kace's school to *Ebony Moves Dance Studio* was brief. I wanted Nick and Darian out of the recesses of my mind. I was overwhelmed with Kace and the meeting at his school. They were also concerned about his anger and wanted to know if there were healthy ways for him to process his big feelings.

My answer to everything was dance, but I doubted that would work for my son. As I stepped through the doors of my quaint studio, my shoulders sagged, and the weight that rested there moments before lifted. The graffiti spray painted on the walls featuring my likeness—and some of my star dancers—filled me with a sense of pride. For a lot of the girls and boys I taught, this was the one time in the day they weren't othered. Dance was our safe space. We could move like us or imitate the style of someone else. We could be more of us or melt into a character of our choosing.

I connected my phone to the Bluetooth speaker and had barely dropped my bags before I let the track guide my body in a much-needed freestyle. *Fuck Nick and Fuck Darian. Fuck these bills and the fact that I can't dance full time.* Becoming a professional dancer was my dream before Darian and I got pregnant. I wanted to move out of Saint Des and see the world by way of one of those traveling dance troupes. I had it all planned out.

Shay made fun of me to my face but supported me everywhere else. She voted for me when I entered an online contest for a dance reality show. I made it to the top twenty but was cut when I couldn't push past my morning sickness. I accepted if I wanted to dance, I needed to do it in a way where I could still be a full-time mother. *Ebony Dance Moves Studio* was born out of my desperation to reach my dreams and raise my son.

The girls who came to me were full of promise. They had their whole lives ahead of them. Whether they chose to dance in their adult years or not was irrelevant. My job was to introduce them to a world where they were more in control of their lives by learning to master their minds and bodies. By the time I was finished with my freestyle, nothing that previously preoccupied my mind held any weight. I was restored to my baseline, and I held a quiet confidence that I would survive anything that came my way.

CHAPTER 3

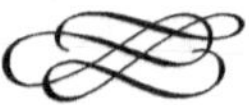

Nick

"What the hell is going on in here?" Cyrus asked as he stepped into my mostly empty apartment.

I was in the process of tidying up Elle's toys that kept seeping into the shared space, despite my insistence they stay in the playroom.

"Don't start, man." I huffed.

Cyrus was familiar with my entire family, including my sister and her kids.

"Where's Jackie?"

"Y'all go wash up for dinner!" I barked, fearful that maybe I was in over my head.

"Dinner? You cooked?"

"No. I'll most likely order something."

I tossed the last of the dolls in a corner, frustrated at how many toys one kid could have. "Jackie's in rehab, man."

"Oh shit. Is she OK?" Cyrus asked as he took a seat in the small loveseat across from me.

"I hope so. She's been popping pills off and on for years, but with two kids, it's an expensive habit. She got caught up, and the judge threatened to lock her up if she doesn't do a mandatory thirty days," I whispered.

"You're watching the kids to give your folks a break?" Cyrus pressed.

"You know they can't keep up with them. I mean, they wouldn't have had a choice if I wasn't here, but I could see it in my mom's eyes they were overwhelmed."

"Are you sure you can handle two kids for a month?"

"Jack would do the same for me. I got them in the charter school up the block, and once I figure out how to feed them every fucking hour, we'll be good."

Cyrus shook his head. "Hit Uncle Mitch up. He loves kids. And he still on me about this damn gym. I told him you would be better at all that than me."

It wasn't his worst idea. "I'll give him a call. It might not be until after Jackie's back on her feet, but it might be good for me to focus on something other than ball for once."

"Have you been to the grocery store?" Cyrus asked. He hadn't acknowledged most of what I'd said, which was typical. When Cyrus spoke up, it was because he had an issue with whatever was happening. If he had no complaints, he said nothing.

I squinted my eyes like the thought never crossed my mind. "How the fuck am I supposed to go to the grocery store with them?"

"Moms do it all the time. Try giving them candy and letting them push the cart while you get the basics."

"And what are the basics, since you know everything?" I asked as I swiped an envelope from the counter to make a list.

"Bread, eggs, cereal, milk, and stuff for dinner. It shouldn't be hard. Most kids only eat chicken nuggets anyway." I didn't know the details around Cyrus and his kids. He had them sometimes, but I assumed the mothers didn't trust his ass to keep them for an extended amount of time since both children were under age five.

Elle was back in my space at lightning speed. "We're having chicken nuggets, Uncle Nick?" Her voice was more hopeful than when I suggested pizza the night before.

Cyrus nodded and mumbled, "Told you."

"Change of plans. Get your shoes on. We're going to the store with Uncle Cyrus."

"Huh?" His head snapped in my direction as horror washed over him. "I came here to find some Saint Des hos."

"You gotta put a dollar in the swear jar, Uncle Cyrus," Eli said from behind him.

Cyrus's eyebrows shot up.

"You can't say hos. It's a swear," he continued as he laced up his sneakers.

I snickered and pointed to the swear jar the kids made me place on the countertop. I may have been out of my element, but they were family. I would do any rituals Jackie did to make them at home.

Cyrus kissed his teeth and pulled out a handful of bills from his wallet.

"That's more than a dollar, Unc. Can't you do math?" Eli asked with a sincere look on his young face.

"If I'm going to the grocery store instead of meeting pretty ladies, I'm going to be doing a lot more cursing."

"Try to use the bathroom so we can head out," I announced for Elle, who notoriously had to go at the most inopportune times.

Cyrus and I spent an ungodly amount of time strapping Elle into her car seat but arrived at the store in less than fifteen minutes.

"You owe me for this, Papa Nick," Cyrus said as we piled out of the car into the crowded parking lot. "Freak Nick my ass," he mumbled, but Elle heard him.

"You have to put a dollar in the swear jar," Elle insisted.

Cyrus grabbed her hand and taunted, "I put ten dollars in before we left home because I knew I had more swears."

We entered the grocery store with the kids and list in tow and barely made it down an aisle before Cyrus found one of the Saint Des ladies he was on the hunt for. Shaking my head, I continued in pursuit of dinner, confused by how women and men did this regularly.

"Where are the chicken nuggets?" I asked Eli. He pointed down the frozen aisle as my eyes collided with Kiara. She was as fine as I remembered with her small curves on display. The kid beside her must've been her son, although they were practically the same height.

"Can I have the keys?" he asked.

"Why? We're not finished," was Kiara's response.

"I wanna sit in the car. Please," he said with his fists balled beside him.

She handed them over as her eyes landed on me and the kids. A slight smile crossed her mean ass face, even though she tried to hide it.

"'Sup, Kiara," I said because she was standing in front of the nuggets. Her breath caught at our proximity. "Excuse me."

"Oh." She stepped aside with a blush etched over her stunning features.

"This you, Uncle Nick?" Eli asked.

"Mind your business," I teased.

Realization skirted over Kiara's face. "This is your... uncle?"

"Yep," Elle chimed in.

"Take your sister to get some bread, please," I instructed Eli. "Regular bread. Not the one with all the nuts in it your mama eats."

As soon as they were safely out of hearing range, Kiara apologized. "I'm sorry. I shouldn't have assumed you were a deadbeat because I'm—"

"Bitter?" I finished for her. She had some nerves to accuse me of hiding kids because she was jaded.

"I deserve that."

I grabbed two brands of chicken nuggets from a sea of options.

"Why the hell they got so many?" I asked under my breath.

"Here. Get the kind shaped like dinosaurs. All kids love those. They're organic too."

I turned to face her. "Thank you, Kiara." I sang her name like we were on the playground. She'd apologized. I could go back to the innocent flirting we'd done when she first cursed me out.

"This thing between you and Freak Nick is real?" a voice accused from behind me. Kiara squeezed her eyes shut, and I didn't need to turn around to know it was Darian.

"Where's our son?"

"He's in the car, Darian," she said with her hand on her hip. I couldn't resist pulling her into me.

Her yelp only fueled my teasing.

"You left my son in the car to fool around with this man?"

Kiara pinched the bridge of her nose. "It's not what you think. Kace got angry like I told you he always does these days and demanded I give him the keys so he could sit in the car. I didn't want to argue, so I let him. Nick is just—"

"Helping my lady," I interrupted. I was having way too much fun for her to blow our cover now. Her body stiffened in my arms.

"Got damn, Nick. This your girl? I knew your ass was hiding something," Cyrus boomed, scaring the shit out of Kiara.

"I'm Nick's finer fraternity brother, Cyrus," he crooned, taking her hand and kissing it. I shoved him away from her.

"What the hell is going on?" Darian asked, bringing our attention back to his general direction.

"Who is this?" Cyrus asked loudly.

"My son's father," Kiara muttered.

"Ohhh," was Cyrus's response. "It was nice to meet you, Kiara.

I'mma let y'all work this out. Eli and Elle, where y'all at?" he yelled as he made his way down another aisle.

"Let me find out you dismissed our son to be with Nick," Darian said through gritted teeth.

I released Kiara's waist and looped my arm around her neck. "I haven't met your son… yet."

"What?" Darian closed the space between us, but Kiara was quick to step in front of me.

"Can we please talk about this later?" she pleaded.

He mean mugged me one last time, before nodding his head in agreement.

"What was that?" she asked when we were alone again.

"Me letting him know he really fucked up this time."

She closed her eyes in frustration. "I was going to tell him the truth about us."

"I know, but what fun would that have been?"

"I don't have time to play, Nick. I need to grab dinner and feed my little monster so he can get to bed at a decent hour." Kiara turned to storm off, but I swiped her phone from her back pocket when she did.

She reached for it, but I easily held it away. Turning my back, I quickly called my number.

"Got you," I said as I returned her phone.

She sucked her teeth and rolled her eyes.

"I promise I don't want anything from you. You don't have to use it, but if he's acting an ass and you want me to pull up to make him sweat, I got you."

I winked at her and tugged on her high ponytail as I resumed shopping.

I'd barely paid for the groceries when Cyrus went in with the questions.

"My guy. You tried to make me sound like a thirst bucket when I asked where the ho… the young ladies were," he amended when he remembered we had impressionable ears near us.

"What's a thirst bucket, Uncle Cyrus?" Elle asked as she leafed through a fashion magazine.

"A boy who doesn't know how to act around pretty women," I said. I reloaded the paid for groceries into the cart, because, apparently, no one else could be bothered to help. Jackie had let Eli go way too long without carrying his weight, but he'd learn in our time together.

"Is Eli a thirst bucket?"

"Shut up," her brother said while pushing her in the back of the head.

"Ayyye!" Cyrus and I both yelled.

"Don't put your hands on her like that," I added.

"She started it."

As we exited the store, Elle continued. "You are weird around pretty girls. You stutter your words and put your eyes up and down like this." She demonstrated, earning snickers from me and Cyrus. "Uncle Nick says that's a thirsty bucket."

"Enough with the thirst bucket discussion. Let's save those words for adults," I interjected.

"OK," she sang as she danced into her car seat.

Once the kids were in, Cyrus ran his hands across his head. "You're going to do this for a month?" he whisper-yelled.

"Yes. They're family, and I'll figure it out."

"Are you gonna call Kiara with her fine ass? She looks like she'd bend all the way over tucking them kids in."

We looked up when Eli rolled the window down. "Uncle Cyrus is an adult. *He's* the thirst bucket."

Cyrus's jaw dropped.

"He ain't wrong," I added, trying my best not to laugh.

"Roll your window up, young buck. And take me to my car, Nick. I need to make some moves."

"Whatever you say, bruh."

Kiara

Kace was back to his old self during dinner. It was a relief since I genuinely didn't want to argue with an eleven-year-old. Of all the advice Darian gave that made sense, it was not to argue with a child. Easier said than done. Kace was between two worlds. On one hand, he was my baby. Not in a coddling sense of the meaning, but my day one who I loved more than anyone in the world. On the other hand, Kace was a mature kid who was forced to grow up as a result of his cohabitation with both me and his dad.

Our parenting styles couldn't be more different. While I hoped to preserve his innocence for as long as possible without babying him, his dad taught from a sink or swim method where our child was to be thrown into the complexities of life to fend for himself without any type of instruction on how to deal with it.

Kace cleaned up our plates without being asked and got himself to bed on time. What did he want? I didn't know what to do with the extra energy I usually spent in a power struggle with my son. I poured a glass of wine and berated myself for the number of times I checked my phone. Nick's number was in my outgoing call log.

Why hadn't he reached out? He said he'd exchanged numbers so I could call him if I needed him. What the hell would I need him for? Why was I curious about this man? There was an 80 percent chance he had his filthy mouth on someone's toes right about now. Ugh. Why did it matter anyway?

UNKNOWN NUMBER:

Girlfriend?

My breath caught. Did I literally think him up? Nick Young had whorish tendencies, and he'd agreed to pretend to be my man. This could only end badly.

ME:

Who is this?

UNKNOWN NUMBER:

Ask the tingle between your legs who it is

I rolled my eyes upward and took a satisfying gulp of wine. My television was set to my favorite show, *I Knew He Wasn't Shit.* The show was similar to cheaters where women called in—and had their men put in premeditated, impossibly tempting situations with attractive actors willing to link—to expose the men for the liars they were. It was problematic yet entertaining as hell. There was no way any of the guests thought the men in their lives were faithful.

Tonight's guest was ready to risk it all for a decoy who was clearly too good to be true based on the lie she told him. I smacked my lips as I considered how to respond to what I was sure was a text from Nick.

ME:

Is this your idea of flirting?

UNKNOWN NUMBER:

Is it working?

ME:

What do you want, Nick?

UNKNOWN NUMBER:

So you do know who I am?

I had to laugh at his last message. I didn't know what the hell I was doing. I hadn't dated anyone seriously since Darian, which was a complete tragedy. Although, it was only right with the way they made men these days. Other than white man Dale and my daddy, Saint Des didn't have a decent man to offer. Naturally, I was parched, and Nick Young was a gallon of questionable water. What the hell? I officially programmed his contact into my phone.

ME:

eye roll emoji It's not like I give my number out regularly. Even though you basically took it

NICK YOUNG:

typing bubbles, delete, typing bubbles, delete

ME:

You over there being nasty already

NICK YOUNG:

It's a habit. Tell me something interesting about you

ME:

like what? You sound like a dating app questionnaire. It's really an impossible question

NICK YOUNG:

Touché. If I'm going to pretend to be your man I should know at least a few things about you for when your ex is acting up

ME:

About that...

NICK YOUNG:

Don't worry about it. Trust me, you'll be happy you have a little more power than you already do when he comes at you sideways

ME:

I guess

NICK YOUNG:

I know. Now stop stalling. Tell me anything at this point

ME:

I bite the side of my thumb when I'm nervous

The idiot on the TV had convinced his girlfriend he wasn't a cheating asshole. I was in shock such a striking woman would fall for his bullshit. *Yet here I am getting to know a man named Freak Nick.*

A smile spread across my face despite my commitment to avoid this man at all costs. I was at war between passing the time with him and running for my life.

I reread his last message an ungodly amount of times. What the hell did it mean? Did they get down like that? Was I okay with their open arrangement? I needed to stop the back and forth with this man.

ME:

> Where are the niece and nephew

NICK YOUNG:

> Sleep, I hope. I'm tired as shit

ME:

> LOL. Welcome to every mom's life. Sorry
> again about brunch.

NICK YOUNG:

> It's all good, Keke

Why did his text message send a shiver up my back? It didn't help that I'd read it in his gruff tone of voice.

ME:

> Are you a super Uncle or something? Why
> are they always with you

NICK YOUNG:

> Damn you nosy

ME:

> A girlfriend should know these things,
> right?

I had no business texting him, but I'd gotten caught up in the conversation. I genuinely wanted to know about his niece and nephew, and I used the girlfriend card because it seemed to have some sort of an effect on him.

NICK YOUNG:

> I see what you did there. *winking emoji

The next episode of *I Knew He Wasn't Shit* started. I'd been swept up with my phone and hadn't bothered to check the time.

NICK YOUNG:

My sister needed a break. I'm not a super
Uncle, just a full time one for a little while

ME:

Oh

NICK YOUNG:

You like that, Girlfriend Keke?

ME:

Don't ruin it

NICK YOUNG:

OK, so you do like it. I'm pretty good with
kids, I've never had them for an extended
period. Thought my dad was in the room
when I told them they didn't have to go to
sleep, but they needed to lay down in
their beds

I almost choked on my second glass of wine. Nick had decent parents. My mom said the same thing to me at night.

I hearted his message and put my phone down. It was time to turn off the television and pull out my clothes for the next morning. This evening with Kace had been a success, but neither of us were morning people. I pulled out everything I would possibly need the night before. I laid out my journal and unrolled my yoga mat. This way, I would practically bump into it when I got out of bed. It was much harder to skip my morning stretch when my mat was in arm's reach.

I took a long hot shower and went about my evening routine. It wasn't until I got into bed and plugged my phone into the charger that I saw the missed text messages from him.

NICK YOUNG:

Keke?

Matter fact, drop your pin

Why in the world would I give this man my location?

I was going to end up on an episode of my favorite show. I didn't follow Nick online, but I clicked on his page enough to see his posts. There was no way this would end well. But again, what the hell? I shared my location and hoped he wouldn't misuse it. I hadn't given out my address in years.

I fell asleep with a smile on my face, knowing full well it would bite me in the ass.

Nick

I waited a couple days before I made good on using Kiara's address. We'd texted once or twice, but between the kids and getting used to my new place, we hadn't seen each other. Her neighborhood was quiet. I pulled up in a sweet time slot—after school and before dinner. It was the middle of the day. Therefore, the chances of Darian getting wind of me making my presence known were high.

Kiara didn't deserve the energy her ex gave her simply because they shared a child, and the more I got to know her, the more obvious it was that he was the reason for the venom she spat at any man who dared gaze in her direction. I had barely put the gear into park when she opened the front door. She leaned over her shoulder and yelled something before she quickly shut it.

She was not happy to see me which once again fueled my taunting. I stayed in my seat but rolled down my window.

"What's up, girlfriend?"

"Nicholas Byron Daniel Young." The scowl on her face almost distracted me from the way her body bounced from her front door to my car.

"Damn, Wikipedia be telling all my fuckin' business."

"You couldn't text me first? Kace is in the house."

"I'm not trying to meet him yet, but you had to know I was going to piss on your crib."

"Boy, what?"

"One of your neighbors is bound to tell 'ole boy I been sniffing around."

She smiled, and the devious expression she wore did something to me.

"Get in."

She looked behind her a final time before she did as I asked.

Once she was inside, her scent assaulted my nose in the best possible way.

"You smell good as hell."

She didn't respond and hardly acknowledged me at all with her gaze.

"Tell me something only your real boyfriend would know."

She huffed and bit the skin of her thumb. "What do you want to know?"

"What do you do when you get stressed?"

My eyes roamed her profile. Kiara was bad. She had a pretty face and a banging body. She was too mean for her own good.

"I dance."

My eyes bucked, and I shifted in my seat, unable to keep my cool.

"Not in a sexual way. I guess most of the dances are sensual, but I'm not a stripper if that's what you were hoping for."

"Who's your favorite artist?"

"Zanaé." She didn't even hesitate. It rolled off her tongue like I'd asked her what day of the week it was. She reminded me of Zanaé a little. Zanaé was tiny, but her energy was ferocious. Both were magnetic.

Kiara's house was at the end of the block within her subdivision. It wasn't near the entrance. Her end of the street location was more of a convenience than a safety concern which, for some reason, was a relief. Since we were parked in her driveway, I saw Darian's car creep up out of the corner of my eye.

"Don't you want to tell me anything about you?"

I leaned over and pulled her face up to mine, kissing her like our lives depended on it.

"Umm, Nick," she started. She wasn't upset, but she was clearly caught off guard.

With my face inches from hers, I whispered, "Don't look now, but Darian's watching. When you sit back, glance to the left."

She did, and when she saw he was in fact watching her, she gritted her teeth. Without any warning, Kiara climbed into my lap and latched onto my neck. My eyes closed, and it took me less than a second to register what happened. Kiara's body was soft. Her scent wafted into my nose with her new proximity. My hands reflexively wrapped around her hips.

My body responded, and she sat back when she noticed. I didn't break eye contact, because I wasn't ashamed of shit. She should know what she did to me with minimal effort. Her eyes were wide, and my mouth watered. We had an audience which only added to the fire in my belly.

The fitted button-up shirt she wore begged for me to release it. So I did. I easily unbuttoned her top and stared at her unwaveringly. Her nipples pebbled under my intense gaze. Any man would be lucky to be her boyfriend—pretend or otherwise. I didn't have time to worry about how far I should go with her—simply for the sake of upsetting Darian—because her breathing and small whimpers egged me on.

I unsnapped her front clasped bra. The moment my mouth connected with her skin, Kiara's hips moved on their own accord.

"You keep it up and I'm gonna make you cum." I pulled back to see her. She didn't say a word, but the fire radiating from her eyes said plenty.

"Isn't that what my man would do?"

I slipped my hand up her skirt and placed my fingers between her split. There was a pool of arousal that added to the symphony of Kiara's smells. She increased her winding movements on my lap. I licked and slurped on her nipple like it wasn't the middle of the afternoon. And once I inserted a finger inside of her, I forgot Darian was there.

In no time, her body tensed and shook uncontrollably. All I'd done was tease her. I hadn't made a girl cum this fast since high school. I kissed the side of her neck as her body came down. When she attempted to slide off my lap, I held her in place. There was a question in her eyes, and I refused to acknowledge it. I would take it as far as her body said I could. I pulled a rubber from the center console.

She snatched it, earning a chuckle from deep in my belly. She removed it from the package and yanked at my shorts. I lifted my ass so we both were uncovered. Kiara deftly worked the condom down my ridiculously hard dick. I hadn't come to her house for this. I'd only stopped by to make my presence known.

"Lift up, baby," I moaned. She did as I asked. Kiara lowered onto me with a small grunt. I almost finished before we got started.

"The fuck you got in your pussy?"

She threw her head back, and I took it as my cue to find her neck again. If she was my pretend girl, then I could mark her to keep up appearances. Kiara lifted and lowered and whirled her hips like we'd done this a million times. The space in the car wasn't an issue. The time of day didn't bother me at all, and the fact that Kiara didn't belong to me was irrelevant.

We were caught up in our moment and hadn't noticed Darian had not only got out of his car, but he was at the driver's side window. He couldn't see much because of my tint, but he'd likely seen more than he bargained for through the front windshield because of the angle his car was parked in. He knocked on the window, scaring the shit out of Kiara.

I, on the other hand, lifted and entered her fiercely. The moan that escaped her lips showed her hand. Kiara liked how I didn't give a damn about her child's father and what he thought.

"Nick," she said on an exhale.

"Yeah, baby."

Her eyes drifted closed and she rested her hands on my chest to steady herself.

He banged again. "Kiara, I know good and well you're not fuckin' Freak Nick in this car."

Her eyes popped open and landed on mine. She snickered when she saw the unbothered look on my face. It was the eye contact. Women were turned on by it, and Kiara was no exception.

"He's going to call me a ho," she whispered.

"Fuck him," I said as I pulsed my dick inside of her. I leaned forward and pulled a nipple into my mouth as if we had all the time in the world.

"You are nasty."

With a mouth full of titty, I said, "You like it. Tell me you like it, Keke."

"I can hear y'all mumbling. This shit is foul," Darian whined.

Typical. He didn't want a romantic relationship with her, but his pride couldn't handle her being with anyone else, especially someone like me. *His fault.*

She didn't stop, so I kept on. It served him right. He didn't appreciate her, and with a pussy like Kiara's, there was no way I would've let her slip through my hands. Darian eventually accepted we weren't stopping, and since we didn't acknowledge him, he left.

I wanted to make sure I gave him a good show once he was back in his car and could see into mine. I lifted Kiara's cheeks and slammed them down on me.

"Fuck!" She cried. A second orgasm made her body stiffen then go limp.

I lifted her to the very tip of my dick and repeated the motion. I finally took my mouth off her long enough to peek beside her. Buddy was pissed. Kiara noticed my attention was elsewhere and craned her neck to get a look.

"He can see us?"

I pulled her face back in my direction, kissing her like her mouth was my personal playground. "You care?"

She shook her head and twirled her hips. Now it was my turn to squeeze my eyes shut. I rested back against the headrest. I'd been so focused on her pleasure that her taking the lead caught me off guard. She said she danced when she was stressed, and it had done her body and her skills good.

"Damn, Keke," I moaned. I opened my eyes and found a half smile on her beautiful face. "Oh, you know exactly what you're doing."

Instead of answering, she said, "Lean your seat back some more."

I inched my seat back, unprepared for what she had in store. There were plenty of women who matched my energy, but more times than not, they let me do all the work. I did it without complaint because pleasing women was what turned me on. But I adored a woman who was in touch with what she wanted and didn't have a problem expressing it.

Kiara shifted from her knees and squeezed her small feet on either side of my cushion. Thank God she was a small woman. She lifted and dropped her ass like she was in a club.

"Got damn, girl."

Somehow, she'd gotten wetter.

"Fuck."

I unexpectedly released on her third drop. As my breathing returned to a steady pace, I tried to wrap my head around what the hell had just happened. It wasn't far-fetched for me to link up with someone if the chemistry was there, but Kiara and I didn't meet under normal circumstances. She used her soft hand and wiped the sweat that formed on my brow then carefully shifted off my lap. She adjusted her clothes and exhaled audibly.

"I… I should get back inside before my kid gets off the game."

"OK."

Was I supposed to ask her to stay? Did she regret what we'd done? Either way, I would play it cool on the outside and hope like hell it wasn't the last time she agreed to see me.

Kiara reached for the handle but stopped when I said, "Give me your panties."

She leaned back and lifted to pull the flimsy material down her thighs and over her feet. Kiara's lips broke into a half smile, making my balls tingle as she tossed them in my direction.

"Bye, Nick." Her lips parted enough for me to see the slight space between her teeth.

My eyes escorted her ass as she got out of my car. And when she peeked through the front windshield at me, I had her panties beneath my nose, breathing in her scent. My fake girlfriend had some good ass pussy.

CHAPTER 4

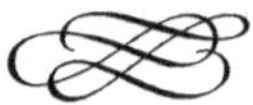

Nick

"Hey, Mama," I said from the front door.

My phone had been going off like crazy, and I couldn't explain the deep disappointment each time I saw it wasn't Kiara. Sierra's Spidey sense must have told her my attention was elsewhere, because she'd been on one. I liked our arrangement and her pussy. Normally I wouldn't have made her wait. But there was something completely unattractive about a chick who didn't let me chase her.

I was all for a woman letting me know she was interested. That was where a lot of Black women got it twisted. Most men, including myself, weren't going to approach without some clear sign we wouldn't get shot down. I didn't care how many times it happened; we didn't enjoy rejection. But once she showed her interest with a smile or lingering longer than normal, that was our cue to take the ball and run with it.

Sierra had given me the ball, and somewhere along the line, she'd taken it back with the way she was blowing me up. She started with a text last night, and I'd ignored it because I was busy getting to know my new fake girlfriend, Keke. I smiled at the memory of our easy banter last night. But Sierra's unanswered text turned into a 'Good Morning' text and several calls.

"Do you need to get that?" my mom teased as she patted my pocket where my phone continued to buzz. My parents had a front row seat to my philandering growing up, but it wasn't as thrilling now as it once was. I loved women more than anything, but living up to this Freak Nick reputation for the sake of not wanting to get accused of losing my touch was extremely childish.

I released a heavy sigh. "I don't wanna talk on the phone. I'll handle it later."

"How are my grandbabies?"

"Working my last nerve. I didn't know I had a last nerve. All they do is eat, shit, and fight."

"Watch your mouth, boy," my dad boomed from somewhere upstairs.

"How'd you do it, Ma?"

"You mean put up with you and your sister? You weren't always as civil as you are now. They coined the phrase 'fighting like cats and dogs' for siblings like you two."

A brief sadness washed over my mother's face, and I was sure it was related to Jackie's return to rehab. It had to work out for Jack this time. She'd slipped further down the rabbit hole. We all worried about what might happen if she didn't get better soon.

I walked over and hugged my tiny mother.

"What was that for?" she asked, trying to hide the water gathered in her eyes.

I released her and headed to the refrigerator. "Shit, for always feeding me."

We laughed, but my dad cleared his throat from behind me. "Don't you have your own place you can swear in?"

This time, I picked up Sierra's call. It was getting ridiculous. I placed a kiss on my old man's cheek which he promptly rubbed off.

"Boy!" he yelled.

"Love y'all," I said as I slipped out of the front door with an arm full of food I hadn't known to get during my time at the grocery store.

Once I was on the steps to my parents' porch, I juggled the contents in my hands and continued with the call.

"Are you busy?" she asked hesitantly.

Strike number two. One of the many reasons I liked Sierra was her confidence. She was unapologetic in the way she dressed and moved through Saint Des, but if she folded the moment her man slipped away, she was not the sure thing I categorized her as. And I wasn't her man anyway.

"I'm leaving my folks' place. What's up with you?" I asked as I dumped the food into the passenger side, then hopped into the driver's seat of my car. Something told me this would be quick.

"I'm trying to see you. I hope I'm not too forward. You've been a busy man these last few days." She purred.

This conversation wouldn't be as suffocating if we'd had it in person. I needed time to get used to my new normal and wouldn't have withheld information from her in a face-to-face link.

"I meant to tell you my time is going to be a hell of a lot more limited these days."

I cruised through the familiar streets of my hometown. Most people who didn't have school-aged children were still asleep or already at work.

"Because of the bitch from your car?"

Strike three. I had no idea when strike one happened other than her pursuing me suddenly, but her accusations were the last straw.

I sighed. "Sierra, are you for real?"

"Yes. Last week, you were all over me, doing all types of freaky shit, and now I can barely get in touch. Now your time is going to be limited. What else could it be?"

Like the low life I'd been during my college years, I considered if I should meet up with her to talk, knowing it would lead to closure sex on my part. Unfortunately, linking would guarantee she'd never stop hitting me up. It would give her false hope.

"I'm taking care of my niece and nephew full time. That's the real reason I was at Rube Foster Charter school."

"Then why was she in your car?"

I closed my eyes as I sat at a red light. *How the hell is she going to bypass what I said and skip to the part she assumes is responsible for taking my attention from her?*

Giving Keke and her man a hard time was fun, but it wasn't serious. Calling her my new girlfriend was a joke. It held no weight with what I had going on with any other woman. My dealings with Keke bounced around in my mind because it was fun, like dealing with Sierra used to be.

As I was set to pull off, I saw Kiara's kid with a group of young boys out of the corner of my eye.

"Shit."

"Exactly. You let her speak to me any kind of way."

"What? Not you. Look, I need to call you back," I barked.

"Don't hang—"

I disconnected the call and pulled my car alongside the boys. There were only so many ways I could play this safely. I was a strange, adult man, approaching a group of elementary kids without their parents present. I didn't even know her son's name. I only recognized him because he was significantly taller than the other three boys, and I remembered the locs. His locs were a dead giveaway.

"Aye," I said as I put my car into park.

"The fuck your old ass want?" one of his friends asked.

I would have been too scared to skip school at their young age.

Plus, there was no way I would have spoken to anyone the way they did for fear the adult would call my parents. I grew up in a time where the entire community raised you and was only a generation away from every adult having the authority to whup your ass when you stepped out of line.

These babies would never know that life. I ignored his friend and stared at the person of interest.

"You Kiara's son?"

His head flew in my direction like I'd crossed his line.

"Kace, you know this old man?"

Kace pushed his friend. "Why would you say my name?"

The other kid shrugged with a sheepish grin on his adolescent face. "He knows your moms' name; why wouldn't he know yours?"

I opened my door and peered at them from the opposite side of my car. They'd stopped their stroll on a nearby sidewalk.

"You're supposed to be in school. It's half a mile from here."

"Spare me about how it's not safe. Saint Des is nowhere near the hood," Kace said with his arms crossed over his prepubescent chest.

Poor kid had no idea what kind of mess he could get into in our small town. Saint Des wasn't the hood, but there also weren't a ton of opportunities for people who looked like us, which meant folks from the north side and neighboring cities pumped drugs into our area. It gave some of the recent high school graduates a job and it made the south side an easy target as it pertained to law enforcement.

"You're right, but I'm one hundred percent sure your mother wouldn't agree," I reasoned.

"He's smashing Ms. Keke?" his immature friend teased.

Kace shoved him in the chest.

"You may as well call her, or I will."

"What if I call my dad?" Kace challenged.

"Darian doesn't look like the type to let you off with a warning. You're either getting punched or working out until you vomit."

Kiara didn't have to tell me much for me to gather they weren't on the same page when it came to parenting.

"Y'all go ahead and message your parents and let them know Nick Young is bringing you back to school."

"Is you crazy?" one of his friends who hadn't said a word until now screeched. "I'd rather get kidnapped than tell my mama I left school."

I chuckled. "Get in. Day time or not, it's not a good idea for y'all to be out here alone."

They huddled which I found hilarious. I'm glad I'd been the one to discover them. What if I was some type of pervert? They had no survival skills to get them out of a dangerous situation.

They finally agreed to let me take them back to school. When they piled in, one of his friends noticed Elle's seat where I'd stashed the snacks from my parents' place.

"How many baby mamas you got?"

Kace sat up front and gave me his full attention like he wanted to know.

"Zero, for your information," I shot back. "It's for my niece. She goes to Rube Foster with y'all and she's staying with me for a while.

"You hit up your mom?" I asked Kace as we headed in the direction of his school.

"Can you please mind your business?"

"Actually, I can't. There's no way I can let any of you off the hook. It doesn't work like that when you're a responsible adult."

"Old ass man," one of them coughed.

"Joke all you want. Y'all need some real discipline. What sports do you play?" I asked the four of them.

"Baseball," they sang like they were a choir.

"When I drop you off, I'll ask to speak to your coach. I'll let him decide if he wants to punish you the old-fashioned way or if he wants to call your parents."

"Shit," Kace muttered.

"Watch your mouth, man," I said as I once again parked in front of the school. My life had taken a drastic turn from late nights at the bar, to multiple visits to a local elementary school.

They slowly emerged from the car and trailed me as I entered the tiny building.

"What's your coach's name?" I asked.

"Coach Malcolm," Kace's most talkative friend said.

"Take me to his class, or the front desk lady is definitely calling your parents."

We arrived in front of a classroom full of equally small children when Malcolm noticed us hovering at his door.

"Nick Young?" he asked brightly.

"The one and only."

His face tightened when he saw his players in tow.

"Look, I saw them on the street, and I didn't necessarily want to call their parents. I'mma call Kiara, but I figured I'd leave it up to you whether you wanted to deal with it the old-school way or if you're like one of those mandatory reporters."

His jaw clenched. "Both. I have to call, and when they get to practice, they're going to wish their mommies were all they had to deal with."

I gripped him up and threw a nod their way.

"Text your mom before I do. I promise you it's going to be a hell of a lot worse if she hears it from me."

"Shit," Kace mumbled.

"Thanks for bringing them to me," Coach Malcolm added as I left the school for the second time today.

Kiara

MY SONSHINE:

Uh mom

ME:

Why are you texting during school? Is
everything OK?

MY SONSHINE:

sort of. Nick is going to text you

I was at the dance studio, making progress on a routine, and the last thing I wanted was my mind distracted with this freaky ass, pretend boyfriend Nick. I'd gotten him off my mind and added him to the not right before bedtime list along with thrillers, because both led to the most graphic dreams. And how the hell had he gotten access to my baby? I hadn't introduced him to Kace.

My palms were sweaty, and my heart skipped a few beats as I feverishly typed my response.

ME:

Baby, you're scaring me. What are you
talking about?

MY SONSHINE:

Me and Carter and a few other boys from
baseball left school

I immediately called him but got no answer.

MY SONSHINE:

I can't talk mom. They'll take my phone

Before I could respond, Nick's contact appeared on my screen with an incoming call.

"What?" I demanded.

"Damn, baby. Good morning to you too. I figured you probably had sweet dreams after our text conversation."

"What happened with Kace?" Now was not the time for flattery nor distraction. Why the hell was Kace texting me about Nick?

"OK, good. Kace told you."

"If somebody doesn't explain what the hell is going on, I'm dragging him from the school by his ears."

"You can't do that."

"I can do whatever the hell I want."

"Right. You're right." He paused. "I was leaving my folks' crib when I saw your son and his friends randomly walking up the street. I recognized him from the store the other day. You know when I got your number?"

I was *not* in the mood for flirting, but it was kind of cute how Nick was working overtime to help lighten the mood.

I breathed in and exhaled just as loudly. I could only imagine what could have happened to Kace had Nick not seen him.

"Where was this?"

"On Second and Baxter."

"Baxter?" My calm tone was replaced with sheer rage. *This little boy thinks he's grown.*

"They were on the good side of Baxter. The other side would have been too far to walk to from the school."

"And he got in the car with you? I'm kicking his narrow ass."

There was no way I wasn't heading up there to see about my child.

"Keke, please don't go to the school," Nick pleaded.

I paused with my keys and bag in hand. "He doesn't even know you, and he got in your car! Why hasn't the school called?" I had more questions than Nick could keep up with. "Are you stalking me?"

"What the hell? No. He didn't want to get in the car with me, but I threatened to call you on the spot if he didn't let me drive him and his teammates back."

"This is a big deal!" I yelled. Of course, I was pissed, but mostly I was scared. This could have gone much worse. What if Nick was a creep? What if he didn't see Kace at all? What would have happened had Kace refused to get in his car? He was safe, but my worries over my eleven-year-old had quadrupled.

"How did he even get off campus? How did you get on campus?" I hadn't meant to ask those questions aloud, but they were legitimate.

"Slow down, baby."

I kissed my teeth. "Darian's not here; you can drop the boyfriend act."

"OK, but Kace is a kid. I'm sure there's a lot they get into that you don't know about. Most likely, they were going to buy a game or some candy. I could tell his friends were little assholes, but they weren't dangerous."

"It's basically the same thing. They're so dumb, they could have walked right into the arms of a killer."

"A killer?"

It sounded bad when he said it back to me. "Or a human trafficker. I don't know."

Nick didn't respond.

"They take little boys, too, you know."

"I know they do. You have every right to be pissed... and

worried. What I'm saying is the last thing a fifth-grader needs is his mother throwing a fit at his school. It's natural for him to outgrow elementary. It's his last year. And by the time Coach Malcolm is done with him, he'll be sorry he ever scared you the way he did."

"You spoke to his coach?"

"Yeah, girl."

As pissed as I was at him and Kace, I couldn't help but appreciate how focused he was on keeping me calm.

"I asked them to take me to their coach. I told Malcolm he could either call the mothers or punish them in practice."

"Why—"

"Coach said he was going to do both, but I said I would call you personally. I also told Kace—who is not a big fan of mine by the way—he should call you before I did. I guess he decided text would be easier."

I blew out another frustrated breath, then the tears came.

"Hey, he's OK," Nick sang softly.

"I know. I'm fucking up at this mom stuff. I act like I know exactly what to do, but obviously, I don't. If I push too hard, he rebels. If I ease up, he takes advantage."

"I treated my mom badly when I was his age. It's normal. I'm speaking from experience. It's like the more testosterone that flows through your little bloodstream, the more you want space from your mommy. Doesn't matter how cool of a mother you are, you represent the person who wiped his ass and pinched his cheeks when he was a baby. On an animalistic level, he is wired to create space between anyone who could prevent him from becoming a man."

I cried harder.

"I'm sorry. Am I making it worse?"

I shook my head. "No. It makes perfect sense, but it doesn't make it any easier."

"Can I see you?"

"Nick," I started.

"Let me make sure you're OK. You don't have to date my ass for real."

Against my best efforts, I smiled. "I need to clean myself up. More than likely, I'm going to hang up and get pissed all over again."

"Which is why you need to meet me."

"Where, Nick?"

I could practically hear him cheesing through the phone.

"I'll send you the address when you hang up."

CHAPTER 5

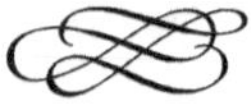

Nick

"Why in the world would you bring me here?" she asked, although the huge grin on her face was evidence I'd done a good job.

"Because you need to relax."

Her shoulders sank. "That's the last thing I need to do. My son is wilin' out, and I'm on a date in an arcade."

"This is a date?" I pressed.

"Whatever. You know what I mean." She pushed me in my chest, and I enjoyed the contact. I liked giving her a hard time about our pretend status. As imperative as it was for Kiara to loosen up, I could use some fun myself. I was new to this world of being a caregiver, and no one had time to walk me through it. I had to figure it out on the job, which meant I was in good company based on what Kiara admitted over the phone. I was out of my element with pickup lines and grocery store runs. A woman's touch was the medicine I craved, whether she was my fake girlfriend or not.

Her eyes were wide as she surveyed our surroundings. I'd

brought her to an arcade with both new and classic games. Kiara was locked and loaded on Pac-Man.

"What you know about this?" I teased.

"Absolutely nothing. I was too young to get the controller, but my older stepbrothers always made this and Duck Hunt look like a lot of fun."

I pulled her into my side as I purchased a card and filled it with more than enough money.

"I feel guilty," she declared as I swiped the card for her to play the game.

"I want you to be in a better headspace before you see Kace."

She peered up at me for long moments. I had no business advising her on the ways of parenting, while I was in a struggle being a temporary one, but I had a ton of firsthand experience with the mindset of a growing boy. The worst thing Kiara could do was to embarrass him at school.

"Everything in me is screaming that I should go and snatch him out of his class."

"I understand."

"Do you?" Her brown eyes sparkled with a mixture of sadness and desperation.

"Yes. He's lucky to have you. I also know you have no idea what it's like to be a boy full of testosterone. What feels right to most black mothers is to emasculate their sons."

Kiara smacked her teeth and turned to walk away. My long arms grabbed her gently before she could get too far.

"Hear me out."

She crossed her arms. The motion distracted my attention from her face to her titties.

"Shit."

With a smirk on her face, she challenged, "What are you really doing here with me? Where's your *real* girlfriend?"

There was no way any man could miss how beautiful Kiara's

body was. And as inappropriate as my timing was—given the seriousness of our conversation—her accepting my help because she wanted to do right by Kace was a major turn-on. As if Kiara had spoken her up, my phone rang. Why I hadn't silenced it was beyond me. The ringtone was a dead giveaway the caller was another woman, and that woman was Sierra.

With a knowing smirk on her beautiful face, Kiara said, "Handle your business, Freak Nick."

Shit.

I stepped away from Keke to accept Sierra's call. There was no coming back from this as far as I was concerned. She was not my woman. I'd been single for quite some time. With everything going on in my life, I needed drama-free.

"Yeah." I huffed into the phone.

"I called to apologize and to offer to help in any way I can. I'm pretty good with kids."

I laughed. I didn't care if she was offended. She and I had hooked up at the club. The sex was good, but to be honest, I'd never had bad sex. Whether she could accept it or not, Sierra was not special.

"I appreciate the offer, but I'm going to have to pass."

"What?"

"I need to focus, and I'm busy right now. I had an amazing time with you, but I don't have the bandwidth for anything close to a relationship right now."

Silence stretched between us. My eyes landed on Kiara's frame. She contorted her body like her exaggerated movements would improve her game.

"I gotta go."

I ended the call and rejoined Kiara.

"Making arrangements with your bitches?" she teased.

"Why they gotta be all that?"

She smacked on the game and pulled on the joystick to the point where she would break it, but still found the time to ask, "I'm ready to hear you out. How am I emasculating Kace?"

Her eyes never left the monitor, and I found it ridiculously adorable.

"He's like a little man in training. He needs respect, which means accepting his choices."

That got her attention. She shifted her body toward me and gave up on the game completely.

"He's *eleven*!"

"I know."

"I'm not accepting his choice to skip school while he's in the fifth grade."

"You should."

Her hands were on her round hips, and I struggled to keep my eyes on her face.

"It's time for him to take full responsibility for *his* choices. I'm not a parent, and I swear I'm not trying to be a therapist, but moms tend to try to shield their kids from natural consequences. You don't want him to experience discomfort of any kind—it's not helpful. If he chooses to leave school, he only needs to be met with the consequences to his behavior."

She bit the skin on the side of her thumb. "Ugh!"

"Maybe see what Coach Malcolm has in mind. If you really want to get through to him, give him extra responsibilities. Does he help around the house?"

She gasped in horror. "Kace Towns? It's like pulling teeth trying to get him to put a plate in the sink."

"He's old enough to help around the house. Cut the grass, take out the trash, etcetera. He's a growing boy. If he wants privileges like a phone, he needs to help."

"You make it sound easy."

"It's simple, not easy," I added.

She rolled her eyes, fluttering those long lashes in the process.

"You're supposed to be pushing me to orgasm, not giving me life lessons."

I invaded her space and pulled her into me. "I can do both, just ask."

Kiara's breath caught, and when her phone vibrated in the small purse hanging on her shoulder, we both sighed at the unwelcomed interruption.

"It's my alarm. It's almost time to get in the pickup line."

"I don't want to," I whined. I still hadn't released her.

"Thank you," she whispered.

"That's my job as your man, right?"

"Right," she agreed with obvious sarcasm.

She slipped out of my embrace, and I immediately missed her presence. I had to get myself ready for Eli and Elle, but all I wanted to do was stay and talk to Kiara. She threw me a small wave, and when she turned around, my mind obsessed over what I would do when I got back inside of her again. This fake boyfriend stuff was really playing with my head.

Kiara

Everything Nick told me went out the window the moment I saw my child. *Who the hell does this boy think he is?* He walked up to the car slowly and got in without a word. I prayed for the patience not to send his head into the window. I didn't make it a habit of hitting my child, but what the hell was wrong with him? He sat there unwilling to speak or look in my direction.

I didn't have to use words; the thick tense air was loud enough for the both of us. Finally, I settled on a genuine inquiry.

"Why?"

Other cars pulled around me, but I didn't give a damn. Why would he leave school? Had things gotten that bad?

"I don't like Ms. Walker's class," he admitted.

I waited. This was news to me.

"Ms. Walker is your science teacher?"

"Yes, ma'am."

Why did this have to be so hard? I wished I could call my mom. My mother repeatedly told me I had to figure out how to do this on my own. I still needed her support. Or at least his father's support. If Darian wasn't unpredictable, maybe I would have called him instead of listening to Nick.

"OK. Tell me what happened," I said as I put the car in drive.

He sighed. "She hates me."

"You gotta give me more. What happened between you not liking her class and you skipping school."

He was silent for a while. It took everything in me not to reach over and shake him. What Nick said stuck. If Kace was growing up, he needed to practice advocating for himself. The only way for him to do so was for me to let him.

"She always finds something to pick on me about. First it was my hair. Then she talks down on me because I do sports."

I tightened. *What the hell?*

"What did she say about your hair?"

"She asked if I was one of those kids delusional enough to think I could be a rapper and an athlete because they all have locs."

My rage had instantly shifted directions. That heffa had some nerves using the word delusional with a child in elementary. At this age, it shouldn't matter if he wanted to be an astronaut. Her job was to support him by putting him in a position to learn as much math as possible, not to squash his dream.

"She actually said delusional?" I tried to keep my voice even. Kace didn't need to know I was on the verge of bussing a U-turn and pulling Ms. Walker to the parking lot.

"I knew you wouldn't believe me." He huffed.

"I do. But two wrongs don't make a right."

"And three rights make a left."

"Boy, don't try me. I get why you're upset. She's wrong to profile you the way she did. I'm sorry this is happening."

"But?" He shifted his gaze in my direction for the first time since he got in the car, awaiting my response.

"It doesn't mean you leave school. With Carter? Together, you two have the survival skills of a gnat."

He rested his elbow against the door to prop up his chin.

"When I do good on the homework, she asks me if I had help. She don't ask the other kids if they cheated, only the kids who look like me."

I breathed in and out. This single mom job was unmatched. I wanted to cry. I wanted to yell and hold Kace in my lap like I did when he was younger. Most days, I didn't have any idea what the hell I was doing. If I could hold it together until ten, I could have a glass of wine and watch *I Knew He Wasn't Shit*. The latest episode was available.

"Ma," Kace started. "Don't call her."

I was at a light, so I faced him.

"Trust me, it's only going to make things worse."

"Will you promise to let me know if she pulls anything again instead of leaving school?"

His eyes bucked, and a car behind me laid on the horn.

"Yeah, Mom," he said with a grin. "We should get home."

We drove the next mile in silence. Finally, Kace announced, "You aren't punishing me?"

"This is your one and only free pass. I'm giving you the benefit of doubt, but in the future, you are responsible for your actions. This means it's not about mama being mad or trying to make you feel bad; it's you choosing to do X so your consequence is Y. Do you understand?"

"Yes, ma'am."

We piled out of the car. As I fumbled with my bags, Kace made his way to my side of the car to hug me.

"Thank you."

"Don't get too excited. Coach Malcolm hasn't doled out his punishment yet."

Kace's face dropped, while I laughed all the way from the car to the front door.

CHAPTER 6

Nick

"What's up?" I said as I accepted a call from an unknown number.

"Nicky."

Her voice was as familiar to me as my own mother's.

"Jack, how are you, baby girl?"

She paused, taking a breath before responding. "I'm good. Tired but good."

"They treating you alright in there?"

"As best as they can. Let me talk to my babies."

"Of course. EE!" I yelled.

"Really, Nick?"

"What? They like it."

"How are they doing at the new school?"

"The real question is how I am doing. Why didn't you tell me about these pickup lines?"

There was a bout of laughter from my baby sister. "I'm sure the security lady and the other moms are letting you get away with things I never could."

Now I was laughing, because fuck that line. I walked them to the door and picked them up the same way every day.

"Is that Mommy?" Elle asked, too smart for her own good.

"See for yourself."

I put the call on speaker and handed it to her, but it was quickly snatched away from her by Eli.

"Be nice to your little sister, man," I told him.

"Was I this mean to you?" I asked Jackie as they tussled for the phone.

"Yes, you were. Elijah, be nice to Merrielle for mom," Jackie pleaded.

"Damn, she used your government names," I quipped.

"When are you coming back?" Eli asked.

I got up and figured now was a good time to heat up something for everyone to eat. I didn't hate cooking. I could make enough meals to get by, but it wasn't my favorite pastime. I'd found a recipe posted on TikTok from a chick I used to fool around with in college. She said her recipes were for lazy moms, but they were within my skill set too.

While Jackie caught up with the kids, I browned some ground turkey and arranged them on tiny hamburger buns, making them sliders by adding cheese. I popped them in the oven like ole girl said I should then added melted butter with parmesan.

"Somebody named 'girlfriend Keke' texted you, Uncle Nick!" Elle yelled at the top of her lungs. I almost dropped one of the trays of sliders trying to get back to my phone.

"It's time for group therapy anyway," Jackie said.

Elle and Eli whined but said goodbye to their mother, shoving each other as they piled out of the room.

I picked up my phone, unable to hide the cheesy grin on my face.

I'd officially blown it. *What the fuck am I thinking, fixing my lips to ask to see her feet?* Kiara used me to get back at her ex, and to scratch an itch she'd been handling herself until I fell into her lap. Or did she fall into my lap?

My phone chimed with another text message from Keke. Her doll feet were not perfect. They had faint bruises as though she danced with the same tenacity in which I played ball. None of it kept my mouth from salivating at the image of her polished brown feet with one foot propped atop the other. My dick jumped up like it was late for an appointment. I sat and tried to steady myself in case one of the kids returned.

She sent another picture that had me both turned on and in tears from laughing. She was bent forward in a stretch designed for touching your toes, sticking out her tongue, taking the selfie. *Damn, she's flexible!* Her head was damn near resting on her shin.

I sent the message before I could add my fake girlfriend disclaimer, but fuck it. I liked texting Kiara, and I hoped she liked me.

She didn't respond to my last message. I rounded the kids back up for dinner, proud that they didn't complain about the food I cooked. Once they were in bed, I spent too much time staring at pictures of Keke and her pretty ass feet.

Kiara

"Why you all smiling?" Shay asked. Her grin faded. "You fucked Darian? Please tell me you didn't let him hit... again."

I rolled my eyes and pretended to straighten the contents on the front desk of my studio. I had a class in an hour, and Shay stopped by, apparently to harass me.

"Girl, please. I'd rather get hit by a car than to let his ass anywhere near me and my goodies." The new smile remained plastered across my face, thanks to my temporary man. Flashbacks of our impromptu hookup clouded my mind, and a whimper of appreciation rumbled deep in my throat. Between Kace and the studio, I hadn't had much time to reminisce, but every night, my body ached to recreate the experience against my mind's better judgment.

It didn't bother me one bit how our little arrangement started— because of Darian's antics. The last time he needed Kace, he called his phone directly instead of bugging me like he normally would.

My smile grew wider.

"Liar." Shay snatched my phone. For the first time in years, I wished I had a lock on it. I hadn't needed one before now. I squeezed my eyes shut, bracing for impact.

"You... nasty... heffa," she accused.

"Huh?" I kept my eyes focused on my menial task, praying it would downplay what was obviously a big deal to her.

She pointed the screen in my direction, showing me the pictures I sent to Nick.

"Freak Nick sucked your toes, didn't he?"

"No!" I screeched. He hadn't, but the way I denied it was as believable as a botched BBL.

"He asked for it," I mumbled.

"How did he get your number?" She closed the space between

us and peered down at me. My bestie was blessed in the height department while I'd gotten the short end of the stick.

I shrugged, knowing she wouldn't let go of this anymore than I would if she sent 'Mr. Trying Too Hard' a dirty message like the one she was judging me for.

"It's just…"

"Girl, if you don't spit it out, I'mma punch you in the throat," Shay threatened, earning a deep belly laugh from me.

"A little while back, Darian was clowning me at Kace's school." The side of my thumb rested between my teeth as I gathered the strength to say more.

"I hate that he gets to be an ass. I told you to let me take care of him for you. I know people."

I gave her a side-eye, but she waved me off, unbothered by my glare.

"What does he have to do with Freak Nick?" she pressed.

I plopped down in one of the office chairs. "Nick was there. He stepped in for me, and we've been…"

"Nick 'Freak Nick' Young is your man? He moves quick as hell. I know Darian is somewhere punching the air."

She cut me off, which wasn't uncommon when my girl was excited. I was about to tell her we were pretending to date to upset Darian, but her eyes were so hopeful I didn't have the heart to correct her. There was also a good chance Shay would never let me live it down if she found out I had a fake man. It was embarrassing. And while I loved my girl, there were parts of my life nobody needed to know.

She snapped her bedazzled acrylic nails in my face, pulling me out of my contemplation.

"What?"

"Why didn't you ask for a pic of him?" Shay clicked on my screen and pressed send.

"What did you say?" My best friend didn't do harmless flirting.

Sis was on ten, always. She tossed the phone in my lap and sashayed to the exit. "You're welcome."

Before I could navigate to my messages to see what she'd said, a banner notification popped up with what appeared to be a half-dressed image of Nick. I clicked the picture in .05 seconds.

Good Lordt! I'd seen Nick's online pictures an obscene amount of times. He was fine no matter how reckless he was. But nothing could have prepared me for the lightly toasted brown skin invading my screen and overtaking my senses. I studied his toned body. It must have been a side effect of his ball playing days. *Not a blemish or tattoo in sight.*

He was leaned back with one of his muscular biceps flexed and rested behind his head. Nothing but a durag adorned his impressive body. I was thankful I had the uninterrupted time to take him in. Thick eyebrows and jet-black hair everywhere, including the goatee framing his lips and chin. My mouth watered, and I clamped down on my lip. His next text covered a portion of the image, leaving a pout on my face. I saved Nick's likeness to my photos then opened my messages, horrified at what my best friend sent.

ME:

I send feet and you don't send me pictures of your sexy ass. I need something to inspire me during my alone time *wink and heart kiss emoji

NICK YOUNG:

I can send more

ME:

Thank you, but my girl Shay typed the last message

NICK YOUNG:

Oh, my bad

ME:

I like the picture though

NICK YOUNG:

Word?

ME:

Yes!

The car belonging to one of my parents pulled into a parking space in front of the glass doors. Relief washed over me when I saw who it was. Majesty's dad arrived early but sat in the car with her until class started. I told him they could come in right away, but he insisted they used the time to create content. The two of them had a successful channel which included their trips to *Ebony Moves Dance Studio.*

One of their viral videos about her spat with another child from dance led to an increase in membership. They could come and go as they pleased.

NICK YOUNG:

I was trying to take a nap, but now I have
a hard dick

I giggled. I wouldn't characterize Nick as a freak, unless he was holding back. He was medium spicy, and I found myself far too relaxed when we spoke.

ME:

Is that a bad thing? Also, how do I know
you're not bluffing?

Another picture from Nick included his lower half. He wore basketball shorts, but his imprint was clear as day. *What a man, what a man!*

ME:

*mouth open emoji

NICK YOUNG:

Now you believe me?

I sure as hell did.

I hadn't agreed or rejected him when the video call request came through. What harm could it do?

"Damn, Girlfriend Keke." His baritone boomed through my speaker.

I reflexively pulled at my ponytail to straighten the flyaways. "What?"

"You know what. You let your girl text me some nasty shit, then you pick up the phone looking like this."

"I look normal," I said, trying to hide my blush. No makeup for me on dance days. Unless I was filming content of my own, there was no need for me to sweat off a perfectly good foundation for the kids who took my class.

He sat up in bed, and the sight had my center throbbing. The picture hadn't done him justice.

"You like what you see?"

I guess I hadn't done a good job of hiding the fact of how much I liked what I saw.

"Kiara?" Majesty's father asked from the door.

I jumped up like I'd been caught with Nick's hands in my cookie jar.

"I gotta go."

Nick's eyebrows lifted, although he said nothing. With each passing day, our arrangement was less and less performative.

"I'm at the studio," I added, angling the camera over my head to include the bold lettering that read, *Ebony Moves Dance Studio.*

He nodded, so I continued. "One of my star students and her father walked in because class starts in five minutes."

Those full lips spread into an easy smile, making my panties moist. "Are you checking in, girlfriend?" he teased. While

Majesty's dad had no volume control, Nick whispered, intensifying
the warmth across my skin.

"I—"

"When is class over?" he cut in.

"In an hour."

"Bye, Keke."

"Bye, Nick."

Nick

The kids promised to be on their best behavior while they stayed overnight with their grandparents. My mom agreed to call if Elle and Eli got too turned up. They swore they were *my* parents, and I was the one who should let them know whenever I needed respite.

I'd planned on using the day to sleep in and stay in bed until Sunday—the day I was supposed to pick them up—but once Kiara texted me and let me see her face, everything changed. I called her Girlfriend Keke to make her squirm, but today, she liked it. Based on the energy she gave during our call, she was also feeling me.

I hoped I was right and hadn't misread her. I showered in record time, returning to my uniform of choice: a blank long-sleeve tee, with basketball shorts, and my favorite pair of sneakers. The weather in Saint Des was unpredictable in spring. One minute, it was breezy, and the next, it was as hot as a summer day. The branch knocking against my bedroom window initially served as meditative background noise, providing the dual purpose of temperature forecasting.

I had pep in my step as I locked up and moved with a purpose to my vehicle. The white note under my windshield wiper gave me pause. My new neighborhood was in an area that was considered the good part of the south side, so a flier on my car wasn't a common occurrence. I grabbed it and stilled.

Nick,

Why would you hit it and quit it? What are we in high school? I didn't do anything to deserve that. You can't toy with someone and discard them when you're over it. Then you had the nerve to have another bitch in your car talking about you sucked her toes. Don't worry you'll get yours.

"The fuck?"

Sierra had officially gone from a sure thing into the bat shit crazy category. I whipped my head around. How did she know where I lived? We hadn't linked since I moved the kids in. I saw nothing out of the ordinary, but it didn't stop the chill that crept up the back of my neck. This was far from funny. I would've shrugged it off if I lived alone.

Without hesitation, I pulled out my phone and blocked her, ripping the empty threat to shreds and stuffing the trash in my pocket. My mom warned me my entire life that it didn't matter how honest I was with some women; many of them would act as though they could change me. Her words echoed in my mind as I navigated my car deep in the heart of the south side where Keke worked.

Kiara's class had only been in session for forty minutes. By the time I made it, there was plenty of time to see her in action. She hadn't stopped sharing her location, which was another indicator Kiara was low-key bae. She rode me in my car like she was applying for the position. A different type of shiver ran down my spine as scenes from that day littered the forefront of my mind.

The industrial complex featured a variety of black-owned businesses. Her marker hovered over *Ebony Dance Moves Studio,* so here I was.

I swept my hands across my waves, only slightly panicked about my intrusion. Opening the door welcomed me into Kiara's world. The music was an orchestral hip hop fusion. Several of the parents tapped their feet as they split their time between their devices and the dancers. The girls were between the ages of ten and thirteen, but you couldn't tell with the way Kiara pushed them.

They were at the bar repeating the same motion. Sweat adorned their young faces.

Keke's back was straight. Feminine power radiated from her and intrigued me like a muthafucka. I had pegged her wrong. This wasn't the bitter woman from the bar. In front of me was a mentor to girls—someone qualified for the title of future baby mama. A smirk danced across my face when she whirled around and almost lost her balance because her eyes landed on me. I winked, earning me a blush from my soon-to-be real girlfriend.

"Grab a drink of water and be back in position in two minutes."

She wasn't mean in her delivery, but her tone commanded them to handle their business. They scurried in a myriad of directions in search of water bottles, while the woman of the hour sauntered my way. I blinked and rubbed my eyes when everyone else in the room disappeared. I hadn't fallen into fantasyland in an awakened state since I was in high school.

I'm tripping. Kiara's hips moved in an exaggerated motion while her pointer finger rested between her teeth. The lights were down, and my chair was in the middle of the dance floor. She whipped her ponytail and shook her ass. I cleared my throat and leaned forward. Keke slid her hands from her breasts down the sides of her body seductively. I was fully in a trance when she finally touched me.

"Nick. Nick!"

One of the dads beside me snickered. I had no idea how long she'd been calling my name. Although she was no longer bathed in the blue club light and we weren't the only ones in the space, she was still fine as hell.

I cleared my throat. "Yeah, what's up?"

"What are you doing here?" she asked with her hands crossed below her beautiful breasts. Kiara wore a playful grin that mirrored her students as she waited for me to answer.

"I wanted to see you work."

She rolled her eyes and attempted to walk away, but I gently tugged her by the arm. "Is it cool I'm here?" I asked. When she leaned in, her citrus body lotion made me want to lick her.

"I guess. Let me finish class."

I nodded and allowed her to slip from my embrace. The dad next to me snickered again, but never took his eyes off his phone. He could laugh all he wanted. I was feeling this girl, and I didn't care what anybody had to say about it.

CHAPTER 7

Kiara

I was having second thoughts. I agreed to let Nick come back to my place. He truly surprised me when he popped up—and other than staring at my ass—he was fully engaged. He didn't pull out his phone once. It was a little intimidating having his eyes escorting my frame around the space. I lost my train of thought a couple of times. It got so bad, one of my students reminded me we weren't supposed to have boyfriends in the studio. The nerve of them to use my words against me.

Kace was with Darian, and apparently, Nick's niece and nephew were with his parents. While Nick's car trailed behind me, I called Shay on Bluetooth. I'd momentarily forgotten she didn't know the full story of what Nick and I were doing.

"Why you on my phone? I know Nick's fine ass ain't getting out of line already," she yelled.

I turned the volume down and asked, "Where are you?"

"I'm at a bar with Sean."

"Who?"

"You lovingly refer to him as Mr. Trying Too Hard," she whisper-yelled.

"Oh, him."

"What's wrong? Spill it." She moved away from the noise. "Can you hear me better?"

"Much. It's Nick. He's on the way to my house for the first time."

Squeals and unintelligible words from Shay. "I'm not hearing a problem. You finally gone get them damn toes sucked." She laughed.

"We already…"

"You dirty little slut."

I joined her in laughter, because when we were face-to-face again, I would give her all the dirty details of our car rendezvous. For now, I only had ten minutes before I got home.

"It's different this time. Kace is with his dad. We'll probably do more than have sex. What if I fuck this up?"

"First, you've come a long way from hating men. That's a good thing, Key. You're too good of a woman to waste your life away watching toxic ass shows. And second, what if you do fuck it up? Fine or not, Nick is not the second coming. There are too many people on planet Earth to be hung up over one of 'em."

She was right. Shay was always right. Her wisdom exceeded her tender age. There were many times I wanted to call my mom for advice, but my girl had my back every time. Between her and my dad, I couldn't complain.

"Who you talking to?" asked a voice from Shay's background. She giggled, and it was my cue to get off the phone before the two of them escalated.

"Thank you, girl," I cut in.

"One last thing, don't watch your show around him." Her phone disconnected, and I fell into audible laughter. I loved that girl.

Nick's car pulled into my driveway, and I swore his energy surrounded me while he was still inside. There was masculinity draped in every aspect of him—from his build to the way he dressed. His confidence was even infused in the style of car he chose to drive.

I got out of my ride and watched as Nick followed suit. He stood in front of me with his head cocked to one side, reading me. I fidgeted, unsure if I was supposed to break the silence or if I was allowed to immerse myself in all things Nick. *Please God, don't let this come back to bite me in the ass. Amen. And sorry for cursing. You know my heart.*

He grasped the bottom of my chin and tilted my head up, planting the softest kiss I'd ever experienced, to my lips. Fire burned in the pit of my belly while simultaneously rivers flowed south of my stomach. Moisture gathered between my legs and my eyes relaxed as I regarded him. This idea of Nick being my fake boyfriend had opened me to experiences I hadn't shared in years. I'd had sex since Darian, but nothing worth a second thought. I wanted Nick… again.

The trepidation I held in the car released its death grip on me the moment Nick's lips met mine. As if I wasn't close enough, he pulled me into him. I'd never met a man who smelled this good. It wasn't an aroma that could be purchased. Nick was a mixture of several heavenly flavors. Hell, the deodorant he wore mixed with his unique musk had me on the verge of an orgasm. I took in a slow deep breath, deliberately memorizing his scent for when he was long gone.

If our time together didn't extend beyond the weekend, I would have at least two Nick Young encounters to hold me over.

"Show me your place."

His smile was devious. My body shuddered as he peered down at me. His arm flexed while he stroked the hair on his chin. The control he had over my body was ungodly. I prayed it wouldn't be my undoing.

He backed away far enough that I was no longer pinned against my car. The moment I turned toward my front door, his body pressed against my backside.

"Hey, Kiara," Angela, the president of the HOA, called out from the sidewalk.

My shoulders sank. This woman stayed in everybody's business. She was how I found out Darian had another woman pregnant. While he was the only one to blame, her messy delivery made the situation worse than it needed to be.

"Hey."

"Who's that, baby?" Nick asked against my ear.

"Angela runs the neighborhood HOA. She's going to broadcast your presence on the six o'clock news." My teeth were clenched, although my phony smile remained.

He released me.

"Nick, what are you do…?"

He loosened his grip then guided me to the edge of the driveway. Angela's brows shot up to her flawless lace front. Her dog—who barked at me nonstop—sat and licked the hand Nick offered her. He chuckled and gave Angela his clean hand.

"I'm Nick. I hear you're on the HOA board."

"I am," she purred.

"How safe is this area?"

The frown I was accustomed to returned to Angela's youthful face. For someone as beautiful as she was, I was clueless as to why she spent her days citing our neighbors for the slightest of violations.

She crossed her arms. "Willow Grove Heights was voted one of the quietest areas in Saint Des. Despite the north side's depiction of the south side, we don't keep up a bunch of mess. We live here, and we work hard to maintain decorum."

"I love to hear it. When I can't be with my girlfriend, it's comforting to know people like you have your eyes out for any riffraff."

I was both amused and turned on. Angela couldn't have been more than forty-five, but Nick had used the very holier-than-thou, country lingo she used when she yammered on at the quarterly meetings. And with the way he'd said girlfriend this time, I had to wonder if he was acting at all. His hands hadn't left my side, despite my failed attempt at creating space between us.

She simply nodded and directed her snobby dog to follow. "He's a major improvement from Kace's father. Good for you, Kiara," she said over her shoulder as the two of them continued their evening walk.

I kissed my teeth.

"She ain't lyin'. Come here."

"I'm already here, Nick." Heat covered my cheeks, and my palms perspired. Why did every word he spoke have to sound erotic?

He tugged on my waistband until I fully faced him. His hands cupped my ass, and I didn't protest. Why would I? Nick could do what he wanted with me. Fake boyfriend or not.

Nick

She let me put my hands all over her. The shit I said to her neighbor turned her on. Those doe eyes kept giving me the green light. So, when I lifted her while we were in her driveway, and a moan escaped her throat. I almost dropped her, trying to get past the front door.

"My purse."

"Remember what Angela said? No riff raff."

I giggled. "My keys are in my purse."

I released her with a groan. Kiara was going to give me blue balls if she didn't let me get inside of her and soon. I'd been watching her ass from the moment I set foot inside of her studio. Now the hurried rhythm of her hips—in the direction of her car— tempted me. It was a struggle not to hulk out and fuck her right here in the driveway. It wouldn't be the first time.

When she made her way back to me, purse and keys in tow, I had a smirk on my face which she promptly returned. Damn, she was fine. Every part of Kiara was as smooth as the lines I would've used on her had we met under different circumstances. Her face was flawless. Her skin always shimmered like she'd bathed in sheer glitter. *Fuck!* Her child's father was an idiot. I blinked myself awake when the front door swung open. I stepped inside and failed at keeping my eyes off her ass as she locked the door behind us.

"You want a tour?"

"Fuck no."

I couldn't take it anymore. Her son wasn't here. I didn't give a shit where we settled, as long as I ended up inside of her. I lifted Kiara, and her legs wrapped around me. She deepened the kiss and sucked on my tongue. The last shred of resolve I had melted. My hands were up the back of her shirt, and I unfastened her lace bra before she could take her next breath.

Her legs returned to the ground as I snatched the shirt over her head. I pulled her nipples into my mouth that day in the car but hadn't had the pleasure of seeing her fully naked. I was putting an end to that right fucking now. She shimmied out of her fitted pants and the thong beneath them.

"Now you," she pressed.

I was out of my shirt and basketball shorts in lightning speed. Before I knew it, I was pulling her down on the rug at the entryway of her place, resting on my knees. Kiara hadn't resisted me once. In fact, she'd urged me on when the sight of her body stopped me in my tracks. I grabbed the back of her neck, lifting her slightly to kiss her lips again. I was addicted to this woman already.

She reached between us and tugged on my dick. If she was worried about not getting it, she could put those fears to bed.

"I want it," she moaned near my ear as she stroked me.

"It's yours."

Her eyes widened. With all the blood drained from my head, I didn't have time to censor my thoughts. It was hers, if she wanted it. I'd been fucking for almost two decades. Variety was no longer my highest priority when it came to women. There was something about the way Kiara made me feel that surpassed the tight grip she had on my dick. It was the way she listened to me, despite not wanting my advice. It moved me when she looked at me. Sometimes her gazes were lust filled, but there was more. Adoration. When I spoke, her listening face was highlighted with adoration… for me.

I used my thumb to stroke her clit. Girlfriend Keke was already soaking wet. Her legs were bent and opened lazily. Out of the corner of my eyes, I got another glimpse of her toes. My dick bounced in her hands, earning yet another moan from her beautiful mouth.

"I'm going to cum if you keep it up," she breathed out.

She said that shit as if it was a problem. The only thing sexier than Kiara's fuck faces was when she was cumming. I high-key wanted to snap a picture to keep me company when she was over this false boyfriend narrative I'd concocted.

I swiped a condom from the pocket of my shorts and willed myself to relax long enough to slide it on. I got a rush every time I was between the legs of a beautiful woman, but this experience was amplified by the fact Keke chose me to break her 'men ain't shit' song and dance. It was an honor, and I couldn't wait to dive back in.

Her eyes were barely open as I squeezed her thighs and yanked her in my direction. Never once did she stop me. She enjoyed the rough way I handled her, and although I doubted it was possible, my dick got harder.

I kneeled at the entryway to what was the best pussy this side of the Mississippi. She pulled at my torso, giving me the greenlight I prayed I still had since I'd actually fumbled with the rubber a little. I pushed my way inside and was met with moans that should be recorded and put on a playlist. I would legit play the shit first thing in the morning and at night before I went to sleep.

"Yes, Girlfriend Keke."

"Fuck me, Nick."

Well damn. She didn't have to ask me twice. I bypassed savoring her pussy with slow strokes and skipped to punishing her like she deserved. The sounds that escaped Kiara's lips motivated me to continue. Her body writhed underneath me.

"Put your feet on my chest."

Her eyes popped open. It was the first time they were this wide. Before my command, her lids were lowered or closed completely.

"You hear me, baby?"

She adjusted herself so her feet were pressed against my chest the way I liked. I went deeper, doing my best not to push her thick frame unnecessarily against the carpet. She would end up with rug burns if we weren't careful.

I angled my head and pulled her toes into my mouth. Her moans turned into hums of appreciation. She reached for invisible shit, and when her hands found my biceps, I winced. Her nails dug into me. I drove into her sweet pussy with her toes in my mouth. She'd wanted this treatment when we met, and I was with what was her name.

Letting her foot fall from my lips, I asked, "You like it?"

She hummed again with her eyes squeezed shut, only her moans weren't good enough.

I stilled. "Tell me you like when I suck your toes, Keke."

She nodded.

I plunged into her wet center, hoping my attempt to punish her didn't backfire, because she felt so muthafuckin good.

"I love it! I love when you suck my toes and when you beat it up like this."

Now I was the one who couldn't stop with all the grunting. Sweat beaded on my brow as I put in work. Kiara could refuse to be my girlfriend, but her pussy wouldn't. We were locked in. I hadn't moved her feet from my chest, and neither did she. Dance gave her stamina and flexibility. I could tolerate a lot, but it was truly a relief Keke wasn't a lazy lover. She was on the bottom, but she'd done everything besides lay there.

I reached between us and played with her pussy. And I'd be damned if her pussy didn't have a conversation with me. The macaroni in a pot line was accurate as fuck. My dick was as hard as concrete. She was super soaker wet, but the sound of her fluids with every stroke had me on the edge.

"Let me hit it from the back."

She reluctantly lifted, and on wobbly legs, she turned and pointed her ass in my direction.

"Got damn, girl."

I smacked it hard, making my own damn hand sting. I couldn't breathe until I was inside our pussy again. After tonight, I would fight tooth and nail to ensure I got it every day.

I grabbed Kiara's ass cheeks and swiped my tongue across her pussy from the back. I had to steady her by the hips because the contact caught her off guard. She'd almost fallen forward. I entered her as quickly as I'd moved my mouth from her marvelous cheeks.

"Nick!"

It was the name my parents gave me. There was nothing that turned me on more than a woman like her screaming it at the top of their lungs. I increased my pace, maintaining a tight grip on her hips. Kiara's pussy tasted as sweet as the lips on her face. Without fail, every part of her plush body had me on the brink of losing my fucking mind. Where had this woman been all my life?

"I'm cumming!" She cried. Her body jerked, and she hit a high note I'd never heard before. Her pussy clamped around my dick tighter than when I entered her.

I held her hip with one hand—as she rode out her orgasm—and with the other, I yanked on her high ponytail, angling her head back until she was close enough to kiss me.

"You see how good you taste?"

She smirked at me, and the bottom of my balls tingled. Instead of responding to my question, she outlined my lips with her tongue, tasting her own juices. I released her hair and grabbed her neck.

"Fuck me, Nick. Please."

Well shit. She didn't have to beg for this dick. I applied more pressure to her throat and gave her my full length. Kiara could handle it. She threw it back at me and moved my hand from her hip to her nipple. *Fuck!*

My movements got chaotic. She reached her soft hands between us to stroke my balls, and I met my own release. I rammed into her three or four more times, shooting off in the condom I hoped was strong enough to hold my seed back.

CHAPTER 8

Kiara

A cascade of thunderous pounds pulled me from the best non-wine induced sleep I'd gotten in years. When had Kace come into my room? His little snores were cute when he was younger, but those snores meant kicks that ended with me pushed onto the floor on more than one occasion. Kace shouldn't be home this early. I craned my neck to see it was barely nine a.m. More knocks. Now that I was awake, it dawned on me the sound came from the front door.

"Who the fuck is at your house on a Sunday morning?"

I shot up in bed. Freak Nick Young was beside me… butt ass naked. For a moment, I thought Kace had found his way into my room like he did when he was younger. I rubbed my eyes as memories from last night floated to the forefront of my mind. The pictures Nick sent earlier didn't do his blemish-free skin any justice. It should be illegal in all fifty states for anyone to be this electrifying. A blush covered my face as I remembered how he carried me to the shower and fucked me against the cool tile shortly after our carpet adventure.

More knocks from the door interrupted my lustful gaze. Nick lifted. At first, I was so distracted by this man's ass it didn't register where he was headed. *Where do they make asses like this?* He almost left the room before I had the good sense to wrap myself in a sheet and hobble after him.

"Nick—"

"You expecting company?" He stood at the door, and for the first time since he'd gotten up, he faced me. Sleep crowded his words. Small indentations lined the side of his face where he'd rested against his own hand. *Good Lordt, this man is fine!*

I shook my head.

Nick twisted his body so the door covered his lower half when he flung the door open. A bewildered Darian stood staring in disbelief. I stepped around Nick's intimidating frame to face my bad choice. Like every other woman in my situation, I never once regretted my baby boy. I wished I'd somehow chosen him a better father. After eleven years, I still struggled to accept it didn't work like that.

"Where is Kace?" It was the biggest concern I had.

"He's with my mom. Is this what you do when it's my turn to watch our son?" Darian's voice was almost unrecognizable. It was wild how he had a pregnant girlfriend and a woman on the side but spazzed over the way I chose to pass the time.

"The real question is, why is Kace with your mom when it's *your* weekend to spend time with him?"

Darian's eyes bore into Nick's bare chest. Nick, on the other hand, was quite tickled. The sides of his mouth lifted, and his brows danced with delight.

He leaned down and kissed my forehead. "Hurry up."

I watched as his flirtatious gaze swung from me to the man on the other side of the door. He all but growled at Darian then slapped me on the ass before he disappeared back into my house.

"I'm serious, Keke," he added from somewhere behind me.

My knees buckled a little. There was nothing like a man who spoke to me with authority. In the short amount of time I'd spent with Nick, I respected him. I would hurry this conversation up because Nick would inflict sensual torture on me if I didn't.

"Are you serious, Kiara?" Darian asked through gritted teeth.

My smile fell as reality once again pissed on my satiated afterglow. "Why are you here?"

"I needed to talk to you."

Darian was a horrible liar. I never had to catch him doing anything once our relationship went south. He told on himself every time.

"Next time, call first."

My grip on the sheet tightened.

"Since when do I have to give you a heads up to stop by my house?"

Melodic thuds from Nick's bare feet headed back to the front sending tingles up my spine. *Aww, shit!*

His body heat crowded me when he pressed his hard body against my ass. "Whose house?"

"Ain't nobody talking to your freaky ass," Darian said. His jaw was clenched, but he could barely face the man behind me. They were fighting to claim me. Darian literally didn't have a dog in this fight.

A rumble deep in Nick's belly reverberated between our connected bodies. "Am I supposed to feel some type of way? Keke doesn't seem to mind my freaky ass."

Darian's fist balled at his side. Kace's dad wasn't a small man, but I couldn't fathom a scenario where he'd come out on top against Nick. We all knew it.

I turned to fully face Nick. "Would you wait for me inside? I'm finishing up."

"I told your ass to hurry up," he said in a gruff tone like Darian wasn't there at all.

I leaned up and pressed my lips to his, instantly calming him. "I will. I promise."

He winked at me, and for good measure sang, "I'm a fan, I'm a fan, I'm a fan," as he turned on his heels, once again leaving Darian and me alone.

Impatience wrapped itself around me alongside the sheet I clung to for dear life. Darian and I hadn't had sex in years. For the first time, I had no interest in him seeing me like this. I was satisfied and glowing. Freaky ass Nick Young was the only man I wanted to see me sans clothes.

"Make it quick, D."

"I love it when you call me that."

I rolled my eyes and inched the door in his direction. "You said you needed to talk to me. Don't keep me in suspense." Sarcastic Kiara had entered the chat. Darian was very familiar with her.

"I miss you."

"I know you fuckin' lyin'." I shifted my weight to one hip and reared my head back in disbelief. It took everything for me not to laugh in his face. "You got a lot of nerve saying this to me. You know Angela showed me your girl's baby shower invitation?"

"And you know there's no love like the love you have for your first baby mama."

Anger radiated through my veins. "Don't piss me off on the Lord's day."

"I'm serious." He cupped both hands in front of his manhood as if it meant he was standing on business.

"Darian. You can't be for real. You agreed to have Kace with me... on purpose. Then, once he was here, you left me to fend for

myself. Do you have any idea how badly your actions fucked me up?"
Tears stung the corners of my eyes. We had watered down versions of
this conversation before, but this was the first time in almost a decade
where he'd initiated a conversation about us being a couple again.

"I'm sorry."

"You're not."

"I swear, I'm—"

"Leave me alone! You love me? Then let me go! Stop
pretending like you want me because another man is around,
because you don't. You like me miserable and bitter. You want me
alone. And Darian, you should be ashamed of yourself. Is this what
you want Kace to see growing up? A mother drinking every night
just to make it through the day?"

His shoulders sank.

"That's what I thought." I slammed the door so hard it shook on
the hinges. Then I was being pulled into strong arms as I wailed
uncontrollably.

Nick

I was completely out of my element. I'd only been this enraged one other time in my life—when Eli and Elle's daddy pulled a similar stunt, leaving my baby sister to shoulder the responsibility that should be shared by two. An anger I couldn't do anything about was hell. At the end of the day, he was still their dad, and Jackie would never forgive me if I broke him in half.

Now that I could finally admit I wanted more from Keke than upsetting her man, I couldn't risk flattening Kace's dad. It would make a relationship with her son impossible. I stroked Kiara's head and back until she fell asleep in my arms. She deserved to be safe. With every sob she released, I swallowed my anger toward her ex. If I gave him what he deserved, I could kiss what we started goodbye. *Fuck!*

I took her back into her bedroom, swiped my shorts, and gently closed the door. I was going to lose it if I didn't release some tension. And since Keke needed rest, I couldn't take it out on her pussy. It was a little after ten. I texted my mom, and she said to pick the kids up before dinner. From the way Kiara spoke to Darian, Kace wouldn't be home anytime soon.

I paced the floor, the helpless feeling pissing me off more. Out of pure desperation, I dropped down and did nearly a hundred push-ups. By then, the burn in my arms eased the tension in my fucking head. Pounds against the door threatened to pull me from my cool state. *I know this bitch ass muthafucka ain't back.*

I was at the door in record time, praying he hadn't woken Kiara. No one was there. This had to be the most childish shit in the history of baby daddies.

"Who was that?" she asked behind me.

I pulled her close. "I tried to get it before you woke up. Would he knock and run away?"

"No. Probably bored neighborhood kids." We'd started having these couple language conversations. I hadn't directly identified the 'he,' but since Darian was recently here, she and I were on the same page. It was exhausting putting words to every damn thing with the other women I dealt with.

I was closing the door when she gasped.

"What's wrong?"

"Baby, your car."

She called me baby. Lots of women called me baby and a dozen other meaningless pet names. Kiara said it with a familiarity that made my heart skip a beat. There was a good chance I was in over my head with her. What if she took her ex back? What if her son hated me? What if she broke my heart because I didn't know shit about romantic relationships beyond the surface level?

I kissed her. "I like you more than a fake girlfriend."

She wouldn't even look at me. My body tensed. Maybe she'd only intended to use me to get back at Darian. There was a chance she'd pulled me in to repay me for what she considered fuck boy behavior. The last thing she wanted to hear was me professing my deep like for her. *Shit.*

"Somebody slashed your tire, Nick."

I know *I pleased her better than buddy.* I could tell by the way he barely made eye contact with me when he popped up. If he was really about the south side shit he pretended to be on, he would've ran me out of her house. *Wait, what did she say?* I was so wrapped up in the stories playing in my head I almost missed Kiara's statement. My eyes flew toward my car. That was when I saw one of my tires was flattened.

"The hell?"

She tried to follow me outside, but I halted her efforts right away.

"Nah. I don't know if somebody is still out here, and I'mma need you to cover up our pussy."

She blushed but quickly relented, disappearing back inside the house. I closed the door and cautiously made my way to my car. My head was on a swivel. I had a weapon, but I'd left it inside of my car. I hadn't been with Keke long enough to know her outlook on firearms. I was going to need to get her trained so she could have one to protect herself when I couldn't be here.

The street was as quiet as it always was. And although I was on high alert, it wasn't lost on me yesterday's breeze was gone. It was almost summer, and the weather finally reflected it.

"Mr. Nick?"

"Ms. Angela?" She had busybody written all over her. She'd popped up out of nowhere.

"Guilty."

She was on a walk with the same dog from last night.

"Looks like you and Kiara had a good time."

"You could say that." I cracked my knuckles, willing myself to focus on the task at hand. Thoughts of my time with Kiara were distracting as hell. "Did you see any unusual cars? Or Darian lurking around?" I was 80 percent sure he wouldn't stoop this low, but I could be wrong. Angela was the perfect person to help put together the missing pieces. While it would be unusual for a man to slash a tire, a woman would have done much more damage, opting to ruin all four and maybe key the car. I was stumped.

With her hand covering her mouth, she said, "Now that you mention it, yes to both. I saw Darian." Angela rolled her eyes. "But except for the early time of day, his behavior was no different than it usually is whenever he's around. He always looks like someone stole his puppy. There was another car I'd never seen. They were driving far too fast for a residential area."

Her eyes locked with my tire as she pulled out her cell phone.

"I can change my own tire. No need to call the police and make a big fuss."

Keke made her way to me, and I lost all concentration. I was powerless to swallow the rumble in my throat. A ghetto symphony played a rendition of "There Goes My Baby." The velvety texture of her skin taunted me. She wore a simple fitted tee and a pair of baggy sweats that exposed her calves and hugged her hips sinfully.

"Hey," she said. She pulled at her ponytail with her scarf finally removed—not that I had a problem with it. She was fine no matter what she wore.

I pulled her to me and kissed her like she was all mine. Kiara didn't know it yet, but I was on a mission to drop the fake from her title and debunk my online reputation.

Angela cleared her throat, and the hood orchestra scratched like an inexperienced DJ with a set of vinyls.

"Kiara."

"Angela."

Keke's attitude had returned. She was so fine I didn't mind—especially when her venom wasn't directed at me.

"Why don't you want to call the police?" Angela pressed.

I shrugged. The south side police would find a reason to make this our fault. It was a reality Angela must've been aware of.

"If anything else were to happen to your property, you'll have a paper trail."

"I guess she's not wrong," Kiara admitted.

I checked my watch. "When does Kace get home?"

"Not until much later. And your niece and nephew?"

"I'll call my folks if I need to. They won't have an issue with it."

We thanked Angela and sent her on her way. While I changed my tire, Kiara said she would make us lunch. At some point while I was putting on the spare, she brought me a glass of lemonade and a shirt. It was a small but moving gesture.

She considered me and how she could help many times throughout this ordeal. Yet another reason to place her in the number one spot. I pulled on her pants gently, pleading with my eyes for another chance.

"Maybe."

That's what I'm talking about!

The police arrived, and I was once again on high alert. I had zero trust in the Saint Des boys in blue. The sheriff blackmailed my auntie's man, Emmet, for just shy of a decade. When Emmet got locked up—despite promises from the sheriff that he'd always be protected—my aunt went to Internal Affairs to expose his abuse of power. Emmet was released after two months, but the sheriff checked himself into rehab, bypassing any real consequences. *Pigs!*

One of the old men kept staring at Kiara's ass.

"Do you have any jaded ex-girlfriends?" the coffee breath having officer who couldn't keep his eyes to himself asked.

"No," I responded flatly. If I could get away without this man shooting me, he would've caught a fade.

He huffed. I was two seconds from checking him about it when Kiara cut in.

"Does the chick from the bar know we're..." she started. She tugged on the bottom of my shirt to give us a little privacy. Everything she did had me ready to go. My head was a jumbled mess. Most of the women from my past were flirty and touchy feely, but it was never this natural. I wanted her hands on me and mine on her nonstop.

"Huh?"

"Has the chick from the bar hit you up since she saw me in your car?"

I nodded. "But she wouldn't do this. Let me send them on their way, then you and I can talk more."

"Mr. Young, what brings you back into our small section of the world?"

There it was. How the hell was I on trial when I was the victim?

"What does that have to do with my car?"

Kiara placed her soft hand on my back, and as much as I wanted to stay pissed, I couldn't. Her presence took my anger from ten down to three.

"I watch basketball. You had a great thing going with the Darkhaven Mavericks. A lot of people haven't seen the level of fame and fortune you've acquired for yourself."

I cracked my neck. "OK."

"If it's not a woman, you could have made yourself the object of someone's envy. It's important I communicate to the team whether you'll be here long term or if you're passing through."

I opened my mouth, but Kiara spoke up. She reached for the card in his hand, giving him her sweetest smile. Why the fuck couldn't she give him a taste of the hostility she gave me the first time we met?

"Nick and I will be in touch. He's concerned and a little on edge whoever did this might come back when my son and I are here alone."

I flinched. Although her assessment was spot on, I still didn't want them knowing she was unprotected.

"We have a car in the area. You're in good hands, Ms. Towns."

The men retreated. The one who took an insane number of pictures of my ride patted me roughly on the back. "I watched the game where you had thirty rebounds against a team from Ireland."

"Thanks."

We watched as the men left.

"Is thirty a lot of rebounds?" Kiara asked.

Could she get any cuter? "It's enough."

"Can you teach me more about basketball?"

"Why?"

She shrugged. I licked my lips.

"Seems like a good way to get to know you better."

I put my hand up her shirt and grabbed her breast. Her eyes darted around her now empty yard.

"I like your titties."

"You would be one of the first," she said, peering up at me with those eyes—windows to the soul she allowed me to see through. When Kiara wasn't verbally ripping someone to shreds, she could be a divine mashup of innocence and temptation.

"Why you say that?" I made my way beneath her bra and squeezed, unashamed by the moan that rolled off my lips.

"I have a small chest."

"I like it. I also like these." I rolled her nipple between my fingers.

"Somebody's going to call those police back if you fuck me in broad daylight."

"It wouldn't be the first time."

She backed away and turned around. I got another glimpse of her hips. "I like that too," I said, slapping her ass to make my point.

"I know."

"You said you want to get to know me better." I tugged on her, unbothered that we hadn't made it inside of the house yet.

Kiara rested against her closed front door. "Not sexually. Maybe I want to know more about you outside of the bedroom."

I tugged the hair on my chin. "Go out with me."

"Where?"

"Don't worry about where. Go out with me."

"Make me."

I looked at my watch. The last thing I wanted was for her son to come home to find me with my head between her legs. I smirked as I pushed thoughts of anything else to the back of my mind.

She had no idea what I was capable of. I pulled her inside and licked her pussy until she begged me to stop. She went on and on about how she'd die if she had more than two orgasms. But ask me if I cared.

I'd done my job. Kiara agreed to go out with me.

CHAPTER 9

Kiara

"Why are you in a good mood?"

I'd been caught staring out the window. It wasn't my fault the sunset was mesmerizing. I struggled with transitions. Summer was a few weeks away, and Kace would be out of school. Him spending more time with his dad got on my last nerve. It took weeks to undo the bad habits Darian introduced to him.

None of that mattered. My mind created scenarios of how I could use the free time. Nick. I clamped my legs together. Now wasn't the time to fantasize, but my lady parts didn't have any couth.

"I haven't seen you this calm since… it's been years, Keke."

I loved my dad. I welcomed his impromptu visits because he was my rock and my safe space. But at the moment, I wanted nothing more than for him to shut his mouth.

"Things are going well at the studio," I said as I laid a plate in front of him and another before Kace.

I served myself and took a seat at the table.

"And she has a new man."

My mouth dropped open.

"What man?"

It was wild how my dad had accepted Darian with open arms. Darian's intentions were pure in the beginning. When shit hit the fan, my dad lost faith in the men I selected. No one was good enough. He'd been fooled once, and he lived by the code that people wouldn't catch him slipping twice.

"Some water head basketball playin' nigga."

"Watch your mouth!"

Kace had no business with trash in his vocabulary, but Darian threw the N word around like every light-skinned rapper on the internet. It irritated me to no end.

As if Kace's foul mouth didn't bother him at all, my dad continued. "Who is he talking about?"

I wanted what Nick and I had to be real. It went beyond the way he handled my body. He was more complex than I originally judged him to be. He adored his mom. He had a great relationship with his family. And he loved his baby sister so much he put his life on hold to take her kids in for an extended period.

Maybe my bar was too low, but it made my day when he showed up at my dance studio. My real boyfriends had never shown any interest in what I loved.

"Keke," my father boomed.

"Yes."

His brows furrowed. Other than Darian, he'd only had the displeasure of meeting two other men. Those introductions happened thanks to his unannounced visits. Bringing up a potential partner was out of the ordinary for me. Gerald Towns had a reputation in Saint Des—and the surrounding cities—as a ladies' man. He unsurprisingly recognized the game men tried to use on me.

We were close, so my dad suffered through several *I Knew He Wasn't Shit* episodes. He empathized with me and all I'd gone through with Darian but warned me against letting myself repeat the mistakes of my mother. Marsha Towns never recovered from the heartbreak at the hands of my father. She'd allowed her anger toward him to make her bitter. We all suffered as a result.

He'd since apologized for his indiscretions. My dad swore my mother was the only woman he ever truly loved. Somehow, love wasn't enough to keep him faithful.

"Start talking."

My dad ate anything put in front of him. His appetite was as endless as his growing grandson's. Tonight, his questions took precedence.

"He recently moved back to Saint Des. We went to high school together."

"What's his name, Keke? Since when are you secretive with me?"

"Dad, you don't like anyone." I hopped up and swiped a beer from the fridge. I kept them stocked just for him.

"And you're bringing out the beer? Must be serious. Or he's ugly."

My dad and Kace laughed.

"He's alright. I would've roasted him for sure if he was busted."

"His name is Nick."

"And dad hates him," Kace spilled.

I wanted to get up from the table and drive to the studio. If I could slip away without being noticed, I'd create a dance routine for the summer presentation. I had a song in mind but feared the girls might find the arrangement too outdated.

My dad cackled. His laugh was so infectious Kace and I joined him.

"Darian hates Nick. Nick plays basketball—"

"He used to play overseas, but he's home now," I amended.

"Hmph. He's retired, and he has my daughter smiling, defending, and in a good mood. I hate him too."

"Very funny," I added.

"When am I going to meet him?"

"No more questions. Don't make me send Kace to his room so we can watch my favorite series."

"Some of the girls in my class talk about *I Knew He Wasn't Sh...* I mean, they watch the same show."

I gave him a mean side-eye.

"There's nothing to worry about, Dad. I know every trick in the book. Plus, this thing is too new to make a fuss over."

I did a praise dance in my seat when he finally let it go. After dinner, my dad didn't stay long. I was sure it had something to do with the alerts coming through on his phone every five minutes. Kace said good night and headed to his room.

When we got to the door, I hugged my dad and said, "Next time, tell them hos don't call while you're with your day one."

"I'm *your* day one, knucklehead. Your mama's my…"

He didn't finish his statement, just tugged on my ponytail and waved goodbye. How could a man as dope as my dad juggle multiple women like a whore? It was a complexity I had yet to wrap my head around.

Nick

FRAT BRUH CYRUS:

Did you hit up my Uncle Mitch?

ME:

Been too busy with these kids

FRAT BRUH CYRUS:

You gonna shack up with the fine ass
mom from the store? Let her be your
suga mama

This dude was an idiot. Kiara was younger than me. If anything I
would be her sugar daddy.

ME:

I have at least six months before I need to
make any real moves. I'm good

FRAT BRUH CYRUS:

Tell your old lady to hook me up with
some freaks

ME:

It's seven am. Why are you awake and
bugging the shit out of me?

FRAT BRUH CYRUS:

Just finished my workout. Don't get fat
because you moved back to Saint Des

ME:

I'm getting the kids ready for school

FRAT BRUH CYRUS:

You're with those kids more than I'm
with mine

ME:

Yeah, you need to do something
about that

FRAT BRUH CYRUS:

I do what their mothers lets me.

I put my phone on the countertop and went to check on the kids. They continued to roll with their new schedule like champs. I hoped the transition to summer would be as effortless.

Elle hadn't asked me any embarrassing questions, and Eli hadn't roughed her up. This Monday was going great. I got the kids to school on time, and I'd be a liar if I didn't admit I hoped I would run into Kiara. I'd practically spent the weekend with her. I figured she could use a breather. My dick and my tongue were at war with all logic.

I slipped my phone from my pocket to text her.

ME:

Let me eat your pussy

GIRLFRIEND KEKE:

Why are you like this?

ME:

You like it

GIRLFRIEND KEKE:

What if I do?

ME:

Are you flirting with me, girlfriend Keke?

GIRLFRIEND KEKE:

What if I am?

Even her texts made my body stiffen. My head was buried deep in my phone, but Sierra clearing her throat got my attention.

Fuck.

Sierra's body was sinful. I blinked a couple times, because it had to violate a school's policy for an adult to have the amount of skin exposed as she did. Her smile was tempting, until it dawned on me the last time she'd made her presence known.

My jaw clenched.

"Not happy to see me?"

"What was up with the letter you left on my car? And how do you know where I live?"

She closed the distance between us. Sierra may have been crazy, but the closer she got, the less I could remember why I was upset.

"I was pissed, but I'm over it. I drove by those apartments and saw your car. It's not like anyone else in this city drives one."

She wrapped her arms around my neck and brought her lips to my ear.

Shit!

"Let's get out of here so I can apologize… or maybe you could punish me."

My head screamed for me to back away from her, but my dick started to respond. She pulled me closer, pressing her fat ass titties into me. Sierra wasn't subtle at all.

"Oh, hey girl," Sierra said with forced sincerity.

I didn't have to turn to know it was Kiara. The moment she gasped, I remembered why my brain tried to convince me not to give in to Sierra. It was too late. Kiara witnessed me letting someone else put their hands on me. I removed Sierra's arms from my neck, ignoring the venomous comments she hurled at my back.

"Keke," I tried.

She whipped around in my direction. I was prepared for her to curse me out. I'd braced myself for my girl to slap me in the face. I expected it since I'd expressed how I liked her over the weekend. She wasn't mad. She was… hurt?

"I'm sorry." I immediately wanted to take those words back the moment they fell from my mouth. They were an admission of guilt.

I hadn't done anything sexual with Sierra since I claimed Keke on these school grounds.

She heaved a breath and turned without another word. Despite her disappointment in me, my body responded to the sway in her hips. I watched until she got into her car. Kiara locked eyes with me one last time, and I prayed she could sense my honesty. *Fuck my life!*

I brushed past Sierra and walked slowly toward my ride with a new headache. Did Sierra show up to wreck what I had going on with Keke? She'd written a letter threatening me. I should have known there was a catch. I sat in my car in a daze until my phone shook me back to the present.

"Hello."

"Young, it's Coach Freeman."

"Hey, sir."

"Are you bored being back home already?" he asked between raspy chuckles.

"No, sir. I wasn't expecting to hear from you so soon. Do I owe you line sprints or something?"

His laugh intensified. "I hoped you might agree to help me out."

"I'm listening."

"We're looking to replicate the type of talent you have in your area and the surrounding cities. I need someone who has their ear to the ground and can put eyes on future Darkhavens."

"Like as a recruiter?"

"I'm asking you to be an agent."

The drop-off line had cleared, and I'd lost sight of Kiara. I needed to clear the air with her before too much time passed.

"I need a minute to consider your offer. I got my niece and nephew full time for a few more weeks."

"Not a problem. I'll be in touch, Young."

"Thanks, Coach."

Kiara

I wanted to block Nick. He'd called ten times already. There was nothing to explain. He was exactly who I thought he was. I canceled my only class and plopped on my couch with a glass of my favorite wine.

The blinds were closed, and my blanket was draped around my shoulders. *How could I be so dumb?*

NICK:

This is the first time I've seen her since you were in my car

I rolled my eyes but couldn't conjure the strength to block him or respond.

NICK:

I meant it when I said I liked you

Keke

I ain't never thirsted over a woman like I do with you, and I don't need to lie. I fucked around with Sierra when you saw us at the bar. After I made you my fake girlfriend, I stopped answering her calls. She's been blowing me up ever since I cut her off. You saw me do it on our arcade date

She left a note on my car threatening to fuck me up when I was on my way to the studio to see you. Doing this in front of you was her payback

I read every text he sent twice. He was telling the truth. It didn't make the sting of seeing her arms around him lessen. The fact that I saw them together shortly after his texts, asking to eat me out again, didn't help his case either.

He waited until she spoke to me to get her off him. Nick was a big guy. If he wanted to push her away, he could have. Maybe he did like me, but where would that leave me if we kept our arrangement up? Would he feed into the attention of any attractive woman who walked his way?

The third time I read his texts, my eyes perked up. Had she vandalized his property?

ME:

Did she follow you to my house?

NICK:

Why you ask that? And I'm sorry for hurting your feelings, Kiara. I should've punted her across the lawn and yelled, "I have a girlfriend named Keke"

I laughed. I could picture him loudly announcing his status. I was still pissed but unsure of what my response to his message should be.

ME:

lol. That's exactly what you should've done

NICK:

My energy from here on out

ME:

Did she give you a flat tire?

NICK:

Hell if I know. She wouldn't have flattened one tire though. Seems like she would've busted windows and keyed my shit.

ME:

True

A new episode of *I Knew He Wasn't Shit* started, snapping me out of my forgiving mood. How could I let myself catch feelings for Freak Nick of all people? Melodic taps to my door—in a baseline musical sequence—brought a smile to my otherwise confused state.

Shay. Sis had an innate sixth sense about when to make her presence known. I stood. She unlocked the door—with the key I'd given her when I moved in—before I could open it.

"Girl, let me tell you about Sean. He is…" Her eyes landed on my disheveled appearance. "What's wrong, Keke?"

One question was all it took for me to release my true feelings. Several tears flowed from my eyes with a mind of their own. The last thing I wanted was to cry over Nick. One interaction had a domino effect on deeper issues I'd been avoiding.

She opened one of my curtains and motioned for me to sit back down next to her on the couch. Shay took one look at my TV and rolled her eyes.

"I told you about this shit. Did something happen with Nick?"
I nodded.

She snatched the remote and turned off the TV. "Why do you keep manifesting *I Knew He Wasn't Shit* energy? Don't you know you are what you eat?"

I opened my mouth, but Shay continued.

"It applies to more than food, Keke. Now tell me what happened? I fully expected you to have a little more than an hour before you head for the studio."

"I like him." I waited for Shay's response and braced myself for her to tease me, but she said nothing. "Aren't you going to say something?"

"I know you like him. I'm not hearing a problem."

I shifted my body to face my bestie. "I really like him, Shay." More tears flowed.

"Keke, you're not making sense."

"He had his arms around that bitch from the bar. The one whose toes he sucked and spilled a drink on me for."

"Ugh. Don't remind me." For the first time since she arrived, a small smile spread across her face. "You let him suck your toes, didn't you?"

I nodded. "And it was good."

"You are such a filthy slut, and I love that for you. OK, she tried to get him back. You had to know he had hos who wouldn't let him go without at least a tussle."

I huffed. I hated when she made sense. "He said he hasn't seen her since we started kicking it, and I believe him."

Shay pulled me into her side. "The dick must have been stellar, because you sound absolutely ridiculous, friend."

I pushed her away. "Whatever. It happened like two seconds ago. I'm mad I like him this much."

"It's understandable. Stop being hard on yourself. But also, stop watching this shit, Key."

"It's not just that. What am I doing with my life?" The tears flowed again. "I mean, I can't use Kace as an excuse anymore. He's eleven now. He's much more independent."

"You have dance. You still love it, don't you?"

"I run a business for girls who love to dance. I'm not complaining, because I'm making money doing service. But is this my purpose? Paying taxes and teaching other people how to go after their dreams. I'm a hypocrite. I'm not even going after mine."

"Ohhh, honey." Shay stood and snatched the blanket from my neck. "Get your ass up."

"Huh?"

"You heard me. You're not seventy. You're not even thirty. This small town has you thinking you're old because we graduated a long time ago. You're still a baby, and if you want to chase your dreams this bad, you have no other choice but to do it. It's making you sick, love."

I stood with my shoulders hunched. There were no opportunities for me to dance here. I needed to train in the off chance one did come. I hadn't focused on routines for me in years.

"So what, to all of those questions swimming in your head. Get yourself dressed—we're going to the studio."

"I canceled my class today."

"Good. We got you an audition before, we'll do it again. Now chop chop, little onion."

She all but pushed me out of the living room. I returned—laughing when she stood ready for a fight—and leaned in to hug her.

"Thank you."

"Don't thank me yet. You got work to do, missy."

I loved that girl with all my heart.

CHAPTER 10

Nick

Five days had passed since Kiara responded to my calls or my text about taking her out. I did everything I could to keep busy. She hadn't stopped sharing her location, but I wouldn't use it… yet. She read my texts and hearted a few, but that was all. No responses and no replies since she asked if Sierra followed us to her house.

The kids were on their best behavior, but it had more to do with Jackie coming home next week. I tried to explain to them that their mom wasn't expecting them to be perfect and that she left because she loved them. Elle didn't understand, but Eli did.

It was the last day of the school year. Although I figured I would have less time to myself with the kids on summer break, I went to see the gym Cyrus's uncle Mitch wanted help with. It was in the same commercial complex as *Ebony Moves Dance Studio.* I went back and forth on whether I should stop by. Since I had no idea what to do about Kiara, I opted to visit Uncle Mitch first.

"Hey, youngblood," he greeted the moment I swung open the door.

There was a group of older black women stretching, but no class in session. Two of the women's mouths hung open.

"Hey, Uncle Mitch. Ladies."

They blushed and waved.

"That's exactly why Cyrus needs to take over some of these classes. Memberships are going to go through the roof."

I stroked the hair on my chin as I took in what he said. "Cyrus said I should do the job for him. You trying to pimp us out, Unc?"

He laughed unapologetically. "Whatever works."

My phone buzzed, and I prayed it was my lady.

"Uncle Mitch, let me take this."

"Handle your business."

I stepped outside and eagerly accepted Kiara's call.

"I miss you." *Damn, I sound thirsty.* But I did miss her and our pussy. I needed them both like a muthafucka.

"Hey."

She sounded out of breath. I swallowed my irrational jealousy about why she was winded. I was sure she hadn't given away what was mine, even though my thoughts taunted me that she did.

"Are you here to see me?"

I smiled. Good thing I came to Uncle Mitch first. "Why do you ask?"

"I see your car."

"You know Mitchell Turner? With the bootcamp?"

"Yeah. The fine ass man with the gray bread."

I clenched my jaw. She didn't have to add she was attracted to his old balls, but whatever. "That's my play uncle. He wants me to help him out."

"Oh."

"I want to see you."

Silence stretched between us.

"I'm working on a new routine. It's kicking my ass, but maybe I could take a break when you're done."

I pumped my fist in the air, because hell yeah. It was crucial that I be in her space again and soon.

"Call me when you're done."

"I will."

She disconnected the phone, and I stood in a daze with my eyes on the lower level where she was until a track I recognized floated into my ears. I turned to see a group of women, well into their sixties, twerking in and out of squats. *Okay then, Aunties.*

It took me a minute to figure out where to put my eyes when I reentered *Fine and Fitbody Bootcamp.* Uncle Mitch taught the class in an upbeat and professional manner. It dawned on me he was willing to play the most current music necessary to get these women moving. The determination in their eyes matched that of anyone pushing through. They were hungry, and I could respect it.

By the end of class, I was eager to help in any way Uncle Mitch asked. The space cleared, and he guzzled down two water bottles.

"It's harder than it looks."

"For them? I know."

"It will be for you too. These women aren't athletes. A few of them are, but most aren't. You must toe the line of not letting them slack without pushing them too hard. Acknowledge their age while not allowing them to use it as a crutch. I've seen them come through the doors lost because their kids don't visit anymore and leave with a bad bitch energy they haven't had in decades."

"Word?"

He nodded.

I helped him wipe down mats and return them to a pile at the back of the room.

"What's your plan?" he queried.

"Oh, I gotta pick my niece and nephew up from school."

"Not for today. You're retired, right?"

"Yes, sir."

"Then you need a plan, son. What is it?"

I released a slow breath. "Hell if I know. I haven't had time to think about it."

"You've been back for weeks."

I took a seat on a bench and tugged at the hair on my chin. "The minute I laid eyes on my baby sister I knew I had to help her with the kids. My folks are too old to handle them for an extended amount of time."

He snapped me with the end of his towel.

"They're not *old*—just not the spring chickens they think they are." I laughed and ducked when he tried to hit me again.

"Could you be using them as an excuse to avoid thinking about what's next?"

My eyes widened. Maybe I'd used the kids and even Kiara as a distraction. I couldn't sit on my ass in Saint Des for too long, but the idea of picking up another gig after ball was overwhelming.

"My coach offered me a job as an agent, I—"

"That's wonderful. I'm not saying you need to work here. I would love it if you did, but the worst thing you could do in a small town like this, is nothing. You see what my knucklehead nephew is going through."

I chuckled. I did. Cyrus missed ball more than me, and it had been over a decade since he played. He used pussy and the drama that came with it to fill his day. While I didn't judge him for it, it sure as hell couldn't be me.

My phone rang, and I accepted it without excusing myself. I would be damned if I missed Keke's call.

"I'm done."

The hell if you are. We just getting started. "OK, cool. I'm finishing up with my uncle. I'll be down there in a second."

"OK."

I disconnected the call with a huge grin on my face. "What were you saying?"

Thwack. He hit me with the towel again. "Damn, Unc. What was that for?"

"Don't be out here in these streets like Cyrus."

I stood and smoothed my clothes like Keke didn't already know what I looked like. "Kiara's a good girl. She works over there."

I pointed to her studio. When Uncle Mitch's eyes connected with her studio, he smiled too.

"Damn, nephew. I see you. Gerald Town's daughter, Kiara?"

I nodded.

"She fine as she is mean. Be good."

I made my way to the door on a mission. "I will."

"Let me know if you can help me out with some of these classes. And this social media marketing shit."

"OK, Unc."

As the door closed behind me, he continued to fuss about stories and hearts and how it made no sense how much time our generation spent in front of a screen.

I took the stairs two at a time. I'd given her space and prayed it was enough, because I meant it when I said I missed her. I slowed down when I got near her door and almost jumped out of my skin when my uncle yelled downstairs.

"You ain't got no game." He laughed and waved a hand my way as he carried a basket full of dirty towels away from the gym.

What a hater.

The door swung open, and Kiara beamed up at me. "Mitchell Turner is trolling you."

They could both make fun of me all they wanted. It was worth it to see the small space between her teeth. The last time I was near her, she'd lost faith in me, thanks to Sierra.

I moved past her, trying but failing to keep my hands to myself.

"I'm sweaty, Nick."

She was worried her sweat would be a turn off, but I didn't give a fuck. I pulled her into me and kissed her forehead. "I missed you."

"You said that already."

I released her to get a better look. "I know you not in here trying to lose these curves." Kiara was perfect exactly as she was.

She leaned up and smoothed the wrinkles in my brow. "I'm auditioning for a part, and I haven't done choreo for myself in years. I'm out of shape."

I grabbed her arm and spun her around. "Out of shape where?"

"Not like that. If you kept working out but then did a pick around game—"

"A pick-up game, baby."

She blushed. *Hell yeah. I'm still in there like swimwear.*

"When you finally did a pick *up* game, you would be out of shape for basketball, even if you looked physically fit, right?"

"Not possible. I stay ready, but I see your point."

She pushed my chest, and I kept her hand while she spoke.

"I'm out of shape for the type of dancing I'll do for an audition and the stamina I'll need for the part."

"That's major."

We stood there in a comfortable silence with her hand still resting on my chest.

"I'm sorry."

"I know, Nick." Her eyes dropped. "I let myself like you despite everything I saw online, but seeing her with her arms around you less than an hour after you texted me nasty shit, fucked me up a little."

"I swear I'm not—"

"It's OK. Really, it's OK. It brought other issues to the surface, like why the hell I'm not doing anything with my life."

"I can relate," I muttered.

"I feel better, but I let too much time pass. I was worried you'd moved on to someone less difficult."

I dropped my hands to her waist and pulled her back to me. "Five days is light work."

"Is that so?"

I nodded. "Let me take you out on a proper date."

She bridged her fingers and placed them in front of her nose like she was on the fence.

I bent and captured her mouth. I'd wanted to do it since I stepped inside. I deepened the kiss when she melted into me. My lips found her neck. I licked and sucked. I found her ear and whispered, "I really fucking missed… our pussy."

She moaned. My hand found the waistband of her pants, but my efforts were halted by her hand on mine.

"I'm sweaty," she whined.

"I don't give a shit about some sweat."

I pushed her soggy panties aside. My hands found her split, and my eyes closed of their own accord. I slipped my finger inside of our pussy. Her leg lifted, and that was all it took for me to give in to the urge to pick her up. I walked her to the counter and set her on top of it. She pulled my face to hers and shoved her tongue into my mouth like she missed me too.

"Damn, girl."

Her phone rang, interrupting what was about to be the most epic make-up sex either of us ever had.

"Hello," she hummed.

I didn't stop.

"Coach Malcolm? Is everything OK with Kace?"

I stilled.

"Oh, good. You scared me. How can I help?"

Greenlight. I pushed another finger inside of her and peppered kisses against her damp skin. Kiara did her best to maintain her composure, but like the sneaky freak she was, she didn't stop me. I tugged on her pants, and she lifted her ass to help me. I removed her pants and panties and only stepped away to lock the door.

"A summer league? Sounds like a lot of work for me." She giggled.

It was irrational for me to be as territorial with her as I was. He laughed, too, and I didn't like how deep his voice was when he spoke to my lady. I spread her legs and pulled in an audible deep breath as I smelled her essence. She put her hand over my mouth to silence me.

I licked it until she let me have my way.

"When would the season start?"

I swiped my tongue between her pussy lips, opening her to reach her clit. She muffled her moan as best as she could while she spoke.

"That's soon. Could we talk about this more at practice?"

Kiara squirmed as she tried to politely rush this clown off the phone. He said something about not wanting to upset the other parents since everyone wasn't skilled enough to participate, but I called bullshit. There were plenty of opportunities for him to speak to her without calling her cell. I slurped and she cupped her hand over the mouth of her phone.

"Nick, baby, wait," she moaned.

"Hell nah. Hang up."

"Now is actually not a good time," she said into the phone.

I pulled her clit into my mouth and sucked it.

"Ummm."

Coach asked if she was in pain, and I laughed.

"I have to take care of something. We'll talk soon."

She ended the call and threw her head back. I squeezed her ass then reached up to play with her titties.

"I missed your hands and your nasty mouth," she sang.

"Coach is trying to fuck you."

Her eyes sprang open, then she peered down at me. "No, he's not."

"Yeah, he is. But he can't have you, because whose pussy is this, Keke?"

I lifted and stepped out of my shorts. Her eyes were glued to the hard area between my legs.

"It's ours."

"That's right. He's trying to get inside this stellar ass pussy. You gonna let him?" I growled as I yanked her to the edge of the counter.

She shook her head.

"Tell me, baby."

"He can't have this pussy, Nick. Only you."

I entered her more forcefully than I intended. Her fuck faces and moans had me beside myself and unable to calm down.

I picked her up and slammed into her repeatedly. "Am I hurting you, baby?"

"Yes! It hurt so good. Don't stop."

I didn't. I loved when she talked dirty to me. Her head was thrown back, and I took the opportunity to latch on to her neck again. Coach Malcolm would see Kiara with a bullseye of a passion mark that read Nick and Kiara's pussy!

"I wanna ride you."

My face was twisted up when I asked, "You do?"

"Yeah. Sit down on the couch."

She was going to make me finish early. I didn't want a lazy lover. It did something to me when a woman could take charge every now and again. She hadn't asked. She told me to sit down, so that was exactly what I did.

I regretted it immediately. She dropped into a squat and bounced on my dick like it was an old friend.

"Got damn, Keke."

I watched as she twerked and grinned because she was the shit. Kiara had me where she wanted me. I tried to grab a titty, but she intercepted my efforts by intertwining her fingers with mine. She lifted our hands and pinned them against the wall behind us.

Kiara finally relented when she released her grip and dropped to her knees. I gripped her hips and met her grind with upward strokes.

"It's the best I ever had," she divulged.

I stilled. Her mouth had me ready to shoot off the nut I'd been holding since the last time we were together. She hadn't gotten hers yet, and I wasn't going out like that.

I flipped her so she was on her back. Her legs wrapped around me, and I gave her the slow grind she couldn't resist. My mouth tortured one nipple while my fingers toyed with the other one.

"Nick. I'm cumming," she announced.

I didn't stop. I couldn't. If I acknowledged the sweet symphony pouring from her mouth and her body, I was going to cum myself.

I gently bit the nipple in my mouth. It was all it took for her body to buck. She dug her nails into my bicep.

"Baby, you make me feel so goooooood," she sang.

"Fuck, I'm cumming with you."

I held out until she lifted her head and licked my earlobe. It was the gentle freaky moves she made that had me hooked. I moved harshly, letting her ride out her orgasm. As soon as her body came down, I joined her in our midday ecstasy.

Kiara

I was distracted the rest of the day, because Nick's visits to my studio were unmatched. I bumped into random shit and wasn't annoyed when Darian asked to talk to me about Kace's summer plans. I mentioned Coach Malcolm's interest in our son playing baseball during the summer and how I'd have a better idea of his calendar once I saw the coach again.

He was beyond proud of Kace, and when I gently suggested he tell Kace he was proud, Darian agreed he should. I hummed at the grocery store, although I absolutely hated the number of times I was there. None of that could faze me after the way Nick delivered mind-blowing make-up sex a few hours earlier.

I bopped through the aisles, singing along with the curated playlist. One of the young girls stocking groceries smiled at me and joined me in the chorus to one of the bops. You literally couldn't tell me shit.

"He puts a smile on my face too," Sierra said as she shoulder checked me.

She was taller, but I wasn't threatened by her whatsoever. She'd caught me off guard. Nick told me the truth. The fact that he'd dealt with her in the past was of no consequence. If I hooked up with Nick and couldn't have him again, I would be jealous too.

I smirked and shrugged. Ignoring her, I placed the items in my cart on the belt and spoke to the cashier.

"You're gonna act like you don't hear me?"

"I hear you. I just don't have anything nice to say."

The older gentleman gave me a nod of approval. He asked if I was ready for summer, and we continued our unhurried small talk.

"You're in a good mood for a girl getting two timed by a man named Freak Nick," she spat.

"Is everything OK?" the man asked me quietly.

I nodded and lifted a finger, asking for a moment.

I dialed a number and placed the call on speaker.

"You didn't get enough, Girlfriend Keke?" he asked. "I'm over here shuddering thinking about how good your—"

"Baby."

"What's up?"

"I have you on speakerphone."

"You know I don't give a shit about that. Your son there?"

"No."

"Then they shouldn't be ear hustling if they don't wanna know how sweet your pussy is."

The man chuckled and continued to ring up my items.

"I'm standing here with…" I started. "What's your name again?" I asked. I had a feeling it was Sierra, but I'd let her explain.

"You know my fucking name, and Nick knows this pussy!" she yelled.

"We can all hear you. There's no need to yell," I added, still unbothered by her attempt to mess up whatever Nick and I had going on.

"Is Sierra bothering you?" It gave me butterflies that he addressed me first. I couldn't be sure if he would acknowledge her at all, but it was the mark of a man with nothing to hide. He hadn't tried to hush her once.

"Not really. She said something about how you were two-timing me, and I wanted to hear your thoughts."

She shifted behind me like a child. This beautiful, insecure woman was having an adult tantrum.

"I told you I liked you, and I'm not dealing with anyone else. When me and you were at the arcade, I told her I needed to focus on my niece and nephew, and when she insisted she wanted more, I told her I was good. I said it as clear as day. I chose you again at the kid's school. Now she's fucking with you, baby."

"I know. This time, I didn't doubt you."

"What you wearing?"

"I'm going to call you later, nasty," I said with a smile.

"Please do."

I disconnected the call and glared at her. By this time, my groceries were rung up and packed neatly into paper bags sitting in my cart.

"Did you need anything else?" I asked Sierra.

She huffed and stormed off in the opposite direction.

"Well got dog. Is that how you women handle confrontation today?" the older man asked with another chuckle.

"It's how I do it."

"Classy. Very classy, young lady."

I paid for my groceries and said yes when the young man offered to load the bags into my car. He tried to keep a straight face but laughed when I said it wouldn't bother me if he did. The entire interaction was hilarious.

"You played her. I almost recorded it for The Shade House, but Mr. Johnson would've written me up."

The Shade House was an online social media site full of short clips similar to what happened in the store. I wouldn't have minded one bit.

I shrugged. "Bullies aren't only people who fight at school. They come in all ages, genders, and environments. You make sure you always face your bullies," I said, feeling obligated to school him while I had his attention.

"That's real talk."

He loaded my bags, and I sent him on his way with a tip. I was officially dickmatized. It would take a hell of a lot more than Sierra's thirsty ass to knock me off my game.

CHAPTER 11

Nick

I couldn't hold back my tears when Jack's tiny frame met me in the waiting area. She wore a bright smile as recognition covered her stunning face. She was smaller than her normal weight, but she was healthy. A drastic difference from the dim countenance she held when I first returned home.

She reached up for a hug, being sure to wipe my face when she did.

"Don't cry, Nicky."

I clutched her. The worry I hadn't been able to process while she was in here slammed into me. I couldn't help her fight her demons. The only support I could give was watching over Elle and Eli's wild and free asses.

"You look good, baby sis."

I used the palm of my hand to dry my eyes. I was the oldest, but there were many aspects of Jack's and my life where I looked up to her. Even the way she made the brave decision to get the help she needed was admirable.

"Thank you," she said with a little twirl.

"As much as I want to whisk you away, can we sit and talk?"

She peered around us and nodded her head. "Another twenty minutes won't hurt."

"What's your plan? Like, how will your recovery continue when you're home? How do we ease you back into life with the little ones?"

Jackie's face was wet now. She cried with her whole body, letting a wail escape her lips that further ripped my heart to shreds. I leaned in and pulled her to me. This was exactly where this needed to happen. The kids weren't old enough to see her like this.

As her shoulders steadied, she snatched a few napkins conveniently placed on the table in front of us.

"I want my babies back today."

"OK."

"But you're right. It wouldn't be a good transition. I'm crying because I love you. It's like I didn't know how powerful my support system is until I checked in. I'm ready to jump back in for selfish reasons. I miss them."

"They miss you too, Jack. I was thinking maybe you could stay at Mama's for a week or two. And after a few days, maybe the kids could stay over with you. Then the three of you could decide if you want to live there or with me until you're ready to move out on your own."

With tear-stained cheeks, she peered up at me. "When did you grow up? And how is this working with all the bitches knocking down your door, baby brother?"

"Here you go. I'm the oldest, Jackie Young."

She elbowed me like she always did when I held back. "Damn, OK. There's somebody I'm interested in."

"There's always a girl."

"A woman," I amended.

Jackie's eyes bulged. I kissed my teeth. Maybe I hadn't been in a real relationship, but it wasn't like I was incapable. Technically, what I had going with Kiara started as a way for me to get underneath her ex's skin. It was real now though. At least I hoped it was for Keke, because it was for me.

"Enough about her. Tell me about you. Other than a slow transition for the kids, what do you need? What was the real issue?"

I swiped another tear from my cheek. Helpless wasn't a strong enough emotion for how my family and I felt about Jack's struggles. I had no clue how it got this bad.

She shifted so she could look directly into my eyes. "There's nothing you did or didn't do. Mama and Daddy neither. Some people's brains are wired to be more inclined to addictions. Daddy worked a lot. Mama ran the house with a strict no excuses type of schedule. And you've always been dedicated to ball. One could argue that we all have compulsive personalities."

She paused as I did my best to keep up with her. Was I afraid of life after basketball? Did I approach preparation for my sport addictively? Hell yes. I worked at the same level every other successful person did. Our dad worked nonstop to afford to keep us from the toxicity of the south side. Somehow, he'd inadvertently placed Jackie in an environment where she was still introduced to drugs.

"I blocked out most of our childhood. Did you know that?"

A chill ran the length of my spine.

"Uncle Ron—"

I bolted from the seat beside her.

"Sit down, Nicky. It's not that. Daddy would burn Saint Des to ash if either of us was being touched inappropriately."

I sat. I wasn't beyond breaking my uncle's neck if he'd harmed her.

"You know how much I loved him and Auntie Reese."

"Yeah. You stayed over a lot, which is why I thought you were about to say…" I couldn't finish my sentence.

"Our cousins were older than us, so most of the time, I hung out with Auntie Reese. I was her favorite because her kids simply didn't need her as much. I loved them down bad."

Jackie's lightly toasted skin reddened, and tears filled her eyes again. "I'd blocked this one afternoon from my mind until a couple weeks ago. I was sick, and since Uncle Ron's house was in walking distance of our school, that's where I went. I didn't want to hear Mama's lecture about discipline, and Daddy couldn't miss work. I had a key to Auntie Reese's."

My heart thudded in my chest, despite the fact that Jackie assured me Uncle Ron hadn't touched her. My phone vibrated in my pants, but I ignored it. Jackie smirked up at me. She ragged on me constantly about how frequently my phone went off. Like I did whenever I was with her, I silenced it.

"Uncle Ron was having sex with Jessica's mom, Tonya."

"What?"

She nodded. "The worst part was when he begged me not to break up the family. Said I would destroy Auntie Reese."

I pulled Jackie into my chest as she continued. "It broke Auntie Reese's heart when I stopped coming over. She kept asking if it was something she did or said, but I couldn't tell her. I brushed her off and pretended to be bored because I was thirteen. I purposefully said the type of things she said our cousins told her to push her away."

"I'm so sorry, Jackie. I wish I would have known."

She shook her head. "No. I learned it doesn't matter what my origin story is. I most likely would have been introduced to weed or alcohol. And unlike you, I would not have the capacity to stop. Instead of Uncle Ron, it could have been being a single mother.

"From then on, I was an outsider of the family. Suddenly, it didn't matter that you were older than me. You still had an innocence about you, and Mom and Dad would have intervened had I told them."

My jaw was clenched. "I'm sorry, Jack," I repeated.

"It's not your fault. It's a relief to put it out there."

My phone rang again, and this time, Jack insisted I take it.

"Is this a bad time?" Kiara's voice was hesitant.

"I'm with my baby sister, but—"

"Oh, OK. I didn't mean to interrupt."

I was ready to run down on my uncle until my lady's voice tickled my ear. She calmed me in a way only basketball and good pussy could.

"She made me pick up. I'm not ignoring you, believe that."

"I do."

"What's up, Girlfriend Keke?"

"I was wondering if you wanted to officially meet Kace. He's been making comments about how I'm hiding you." She laughed, and the light, nervous inflections in her voice made my pulse accelerate. I stood to create space between Jack and me.

"You sure about this?"

"If it's too soon or too much…"

"I want to. *He* doesn't want me around though. The last time he saw me, I was taking him back to school."

"I figured a rip the bandage approach would make having you around easier. You stopping by on weekends is like me hiding you."

I had a big grin on my face. "I'm your man for real now." This had moved beyond a situationship.

"Maybe."

"I wasn't asking, Keke."

A silence stretched between us. I swung my head in my sister's direction and saw her smirking at me.

"I gotta go. Give me a beat to get the kids settled now that my sister's back, and we'll figure out when to make it happen."

"I find that very attractive."

I would have a hard dick if she kept it up. It wasn't like she'd said anything crazy. Kiara was mild compared to what I was used to, yet my body responded to her easily.

"What I do?" Curiosity had me ready to take a trip down a rabbit hole, no matter where I was.

"The care you have for your family turns me on."

"Is that right?"

"Yes."

She moaned the word, and sensations traveled from my ear to my bouncing dick.

"You play too much. I'll talk to you later."

"Bye, Nick."

I disconnected the call and counted to ten. *Sheesh!*

I cracked my neck and my thumbs and slowly made my way back to where Jackie was seated.

She eyed me suspiciously. "You really like this one."

"Don't start."

"When can I meet her?"

I stood, dodging her question. "Is this your only bag?"

"Yep."

She said goodbye to some of the employees who reminded her about the daily online meetings they expected her to attend along with the weekly counseling sessions. Jackie didn't push me about Kiara. We spent the ride home talking about how to prepare the kids for summer and the recovering version of their mom.

Kiara

Kace had an attitude. I told him Nick would be here soon. We'd been doing our thing for over two months, with the last two weeks as an actual couple. So far, he'd only been to the house when Kace was with Darian. It was hilarious how Darian didn't give me any shit these days, just as Nick predicted.

I spearheaded this whole thing, and now I had second thoughts. Nick, on the other hand, had lost the patience to sneak around. I wanted them both happy. With all the addictive dick he'd been throwing my way, I would do almost anything to keep it—including this potentially explosive meeting to ensure Nick could get along with my son.

"Stop slamming your door, Kace."

He reopened his door and closed it softly with more drama than I'd known him to use. I sighed. Maybe I should call this whole thing off. My time with Kace was already limited. I would look up and he'd be a teenager no longer interested in his mother. There would be little I could do to prevent him from moving in with his dad full time.

"Why is this big head man coming to our house?"

I fought to hold in my laughter. He was serious. I threw away trash from our lunch. Once Kace finished the school year, all I did was cook.

"I told you his name is Nick."

"Freak Nick."

I whipped around to face him.

"I saw his social media."

Another area his father and I didn't agree on. I tucked my lips between my teeth to keep from screaming. Nick's online persona was intense. There was no way of watering it down. It certainly wasn't appropriate for kids.

"I didn't look him up. I saw it on dad's phone. He's been mumbling about this dude for days now."

"OK. Your father and I don't need to like who the other dates. I want you to meet him because he may be around more often."

Kace huffed as a knock sounded on the door.

"He'll only be here for a short visit since you have baseball practice."

He gave me a slight nod, and I wandered to the front door.

I smelled him before he stepped inside. I loved a good beard like the next woman, but Nick's goatee made my lady parts percolate.

"Hey," he said as he leaned down and pulled me into a hug.

"Hey."

Kace stood against the opposite doorframe with his arms crossed. I swear this boy thought he was my daddy.

"Kace, this is Nick."

"We met," he growled.

"What's up, Kace?"

Kace nodded but didn't bother greeting my guest. I wouldn't force a connection between the two of them, but I really hoped he would warm up to him.

"Can I go now?" my son asked. I wanted to say, 'hell no,' but would only cause more tension if I did.

"We're leaving for practice at five forty-five. Coach Malcolm says you can't be late to practice."

"OK, Ma."

He bopped out of the room.

"Be ready to get in the car at five forty-five, Kace. I'm not playing."

I plopped down on the couch. *I need a vacation.* When I looked up, a pair of hypnotic eyes twinkled in my direction.

"What?" I asked. This man made me blush like a schoolgirl.

"You. I'm happy to see you."

I smiled. "How's Jackie?"

Nick's body tightened at the mention of his sister, and I wished I hadn't brought it up. She'd gotten out of rehab, and he hadn't said much else since.

"She's doing good, given the circumstances. The kids barely let her out of their sight."

He chuckled, but there was more to the story than he let on. We sat quietly.

"I figured a short first visit would be best. I've never done this."

"It shows. This could've gone a lot worse." He scooted closer to me and grabbed the remote.

"What are you doing?"

"Sewing a blanket. What does it look like?" he teased. The familiar sounds of squeaky sneakers and commentators emitted from the television. He and Kace had a lot in common. Darian wasn't into sports. He liked the lifestyle sports provided the athletes, but it wasn't his thing. Kace begged him to watch, but he mostly played with his phone beside Kace.

Nick tugged on my ponytail. "You got any beer?"

I rolled my eyes and stood. They were for my dad because I sure as hell didn't drink it. I rummaged through the drawers for the bottle opener when Kace's voice stopped me in my tracks.

"The Darkhavens made the playoffs?"

I watched as Nick stared at Kace for long moments. "Yeah. You keep up with the international teams?"

Kace nodded. "Stevens is a beast. He joined the league after high school. Everybody knows him."

Kace took a seat on the opposite side of the room from Nick. His eyes were glued to the TV. They spoke about statistics I couldn't comprehend. I was proud of my son. His knowledge of sports was beyond impressive. From where I stood, those numbers sounded like complicated math.

I handed Nick the opened beer while they chatted about who was out due to injury.

"Thank you, baby," Nick said as he threw me a wink then returned his attention to the game.

My insides liquified. A man this fine engulfed in a refreshing conversation with my son was an absolute turn-on. I returned to the kitchen to busy myself from the fact I couldn't wait to get Nick's dick in my mouth. Shay was right. I was a filthy slut.

I'd gathered the trash and had my hand against the doorknob when Nick's voice startled the shit out of me.

"What are you doing?"

I opened my mouth to respond, but he continued.

"Did your mom cook for you today?"

"Yeah," Kace said as he shifted in his seat. He chewed on his lip like he did whenever he was nervous.

Nick stared at him blankly.

"Yes," Kace amended.

"Then why the hell is she taking out the trash, man?"

"Nick—"

He gave me a look that both turned me on and scared me a little.

Kace stood and quickly hustled in my direction. He grabbed the trash from me and took it outside. I was speechless. The number of times I'd nagged this boy to help me around the house was unfathomable, yet Nick said less than a handful of words, and Kace responded positively. I was blessed Kace had his father, but it was apparent he needed a strong male role model in his life as desperately as I wanted Nick in my bed.

Nick's eyes had refocused on the game.

"How did you do that?"

He shrugged. "Kids need structure—especially boys. It's like moms are satisfied with their sons loving them."

My hand found my hip. "Are you saying loving me is a bad thing?"

"I'm saying that's not enough. We aren't wired to want love. We need respect. It means more when a man gives you their respect."

I frowned. He angled his body to face me.

"Men have to work hard to love a woman. But a boy will use love to manipulate their mother. You have to demand his respect so he knows what he deserves, and he, in turn, treats people right. A disrespectful man is of no use to anyone."

Why did every word he spoke sound erotic? As uncomfortable as his declaration made me, in my gut, I was sure he was right.

Kace bopped back into the house and placed a kiss on my cheek. "Thanks for lunch, Mama."

I muffled a gasp. "You're welcome, son."

He hustled to the bathroom to wash his hands then scrambled back to the couch to finish the game with my new man.

CHAPTER 12

Kiara

"Can you believe we're finally here?" Shay asked with her head practically hanging out of the rideshare window.

"We take this trip every summer," I fussed. I wanted nothing more than to spend our annual girls' trip by the beach for seven days. But being away from Kace and Nick for this long put me in a bit of a sullen mood. When my life was all frustration with Darian's and Kace's tempers, I had to get away.

These days, Kace was showing me respect. He asked how he could help instead of waiting for me to beg him. And Nick Young had me dick whipped. I quivered at the thought of what his mouth did.

The Midnight Sands Resort and Spa came into view. Despite my initial reticence, my shoulders relaxed, and I remembered why we planned these getaways.

Nick

Kiara had been gone for three days, and I was beside myself. I'd been up under my mom and sister so long I'd started saying phrases like beside myself. Cyrus dragged me out to the same bar where I first met Kiara, and my family encouraged his fraternal behavior. They said I was too uptight. Little did they know, it had more to do with the fact that I missed my girl and her damn toes.

Here I was with a scowl tattooed on my face. Being posted up at the bar only reminded me of her more.

"Yo, they were right. Zanaé's up in here!" Cyrus yelled.

Zanaé and I flirted back and forth on social media last year. I'd only met her twice, and neither time seemed right for me to make a move. I wouldn't go out like a groupie. What I look like? The last I saw, she'd posted a male friend who was probably her man.

The crowd parted, and she stepped next to me where I sat pouting.

"She must be real special!" Zanaé yelled next to my ear.

She wasn't the only one who'd been a simp online. When Kiara left for her vacation, I wasn't happy. It was a girls' trip. I'd knocked off a few women who were on one of those for the sole purpose to get their lick back under the guise of it being a time to hang out with the girls. Even though I was salty as hell, I posted a pic of me on her couch with her feet on my face. It was shortly after we'd had some of the best sex of my life. The goofy grin on my face—or what you could see of it—said as much.

The caption simply read, *"I f*ck with her heavy"* #girlfriend. In less than an hour, it had over nine thousand likes and a bunch of comments and shares. She DM'd me a pair of eyes emoji and a water droplet emoji.

"About as special as your *friend*." I added emphasis to the word friend, letting my eyebrows bounce up and down.

She elbowed me. "I'm happy for you, Nick. It was time for you to slow down, and I was not the woman for the job. All I would have done was presented you with even more ass." Zanaé laughed and leaned in, touching me in the harmless yet flirtatious way she always did.

"Like now? You know standing this close is going to get me dragged into some shit. Move." I pushed her playfully. Her muscle was in my space in no time.

"He's joking, Goliath." She stepped between us, and I held my hands in the air.

"Zanaé, I'm being a bad friend."

"Yeah, you are," Cyrus agreed.

"This is my homeboy Cyrus."

Zanaé shook his hand, and this silly man almost fainted. "I have to get going, but it was nice seeing you, Nick. Stay out of trouble if you really like her." She leaned up, but I dogged her hug, shifting her to face Cyrus. She obliged and embraced him with a smile.

"It was nice to meet you."

With one last wave, Zanaé was gone, and the crowd that had gathered around us dispersed.

My brief conversation with the pop princess herself put me back in good spirits. Talking about Kiara with someone other than my friends and family made it real. I opened my phone and located Keke's exact location.

I booked a flight for the Midnight Sands Resort and Spa for first thing in the morning.

Kiara

"Girl, look at this," Shay said. Her voice echoed around our pristine suite. It was as large as a one-story home. I couldn't shake the feeling I was being watched. Along with *I Knew He Wasn't Shit,* I had a bad habit of watching videos of people being attacked.

A chill crept up my spine as a thud rang out somewhere near the entrance of our unit. I jumped, startling Shay.

"Did you hear that?"

"Yes, but it's probably a guest who drank too much." She waved her hand and returned her attention to the screen of her phone. "Your man is trending online, and this shit is hilarious."

My stomach dropped. I'd completely forgotten about the strange sound and how I'd been uneasy since we arrived a few days ago. My worst fear hung in the air between me and my best friend's phone. Nick fucking up wouldn't be funny to me. To Shay, anyone could get roasted.

She aimed the phone in my direction. I braced myself to ghost him like I'd done after Sierra had her whorish hands on him, but this time, it would be for good. It was a fifteen second clip—posted by an online gossip site—of Nick with my shero Zanaé.

The mimosas we had earlier threatened to reemerge as I reeled over having to fight a megastar over my man. Who was I kidding? There was no way I could compete with her, even if I wanted to. Zanaé was stunning. She could sing, dance, and act. And she was everybody's woman crush all the damn days.

I blinked to make sure I saw what I thought I did. A giggle escaped my lips as I watched Nick do a spin move on Zanaé to dodge her embrace. Instead, she hugged his friend who clearly had a thing for her.

"You tamed Freak Nick?"

I shrugged. Had I?

When a knock sounded at the door, I yelped.

"Girl, you're freaking me out. Maybe it's room service or that fine man I saw at the bar."

I stood and was on her heels. "I didn't order anything. Did you? And I know you didn't tell a strange man where we're laying our heads at night."

Shay spun around to face me.

"Listen, princess. I'm a single woman who lives on the south side of Saint Des. I ain't giving no one my location. But you've got to try and relax." She turned back toward the door and added, "Take one of those gummies."

I lived on the south side too. Technically, I lived on the cusp of the north side, but still. I did most of my daily tasks alone, and I was never this bothered. Something was off at this resort—I couldn't figure out what it was.

Shay peeked through the peephole and kissed her teeth. She rolled her eyes at me then opened the door with her hand on her hip.

"How did you find us?"

"Hello to you too, Shayla."

It was him. I hustled around my friend and jumped into his arms.

"Damn, baby. You missed me?"

Tears welled in my eyes. I hadn't been safe until this moment. I would have to figure out how to talk Shay into letting him stay, but this was the best surprise I'd ever gotten.

"How are you here?" I asked between sniffs.

"How *are* you here? Don't let me find out you a stalker," Shay added as she pulled out a water bottle from the fridge.

He grabbed a small bag and walked me inside, closing the door behind him. With his eyes still locked on mine, he lowered me to my feet and responded, "You never stopped sharing your location, and I missed you."

Nick's voice was deeper than usual. The goatee that made my center pulse was on full display.

"Ugh. Y'all are disgustingly cute. I'm going to bed. Don't wake me up."

I mugged Shay who simply stuck out her tongue at me.

"Our beds are on completely different sides of the suite," I said.

"Maybe this time you'll stay in your own room, heffa."

She waved and disappeared to her side of the room.

Nick pulled me in and kissed me until I was lightheaded. "Damn, you taste good. You been drinking without me?"

"You been clubbing without me?"

I crossed my arms and cocked my head to the side.

"Zanaé is not an issue. I ain't seeing nobody but you."

The sincerity in his words made me feel like a jerk for teasing him. I walked away from him to get my phone. I didn't miss the 'Damn,' he tried but failed to mumble at my backside.

I retrieved my phone and pulled up the video Shay showed me.

He rubbed a hand down his freshly cut waves. "Zanaé and I went back and forth on socials, but we never hooked up. People are crafting fake news ever since I posted your feet pic."

He smirked at the mention of my feet, but I kept my face even. "Explain this."

He looked at the screen then back up at me. "Oh, you got jokes?"

I giggled and ran from him, only making it a few steps before he swooped me up. "I needed to see you, so I booked a flight at the bar right after I pump faked her."

I stared into his eyes, searching for an iota of game but saw none. "Are you done with the whole Freak Nick persona?"

"Hell nah. Freak Nick is about to show out right fucking now. I'm horny as hell, Keke."

My nipples hardened beneath the beater I wore. My body ached for him each night I'd been here. I prayed he would provide the relief I'd dreamt of while we were apart.

"Show me the shower."

I led him to my side of the suite where the large spa bathroom was adjoined to the bedroom. I'd attempted to sleep here the first night but was spooked by strange noises. Shay assured me it was the animals who lived near the beach. Luckily, she didn't have a problem sharing a bed with me since the mattress could easily fit a group of four.

I sat on the bed and watched him move around. Nick took his shoes off and neatly pushed them against a wall in the corner. He emptied his pocket of his wallet and phone with my eyes never leaving his imposing frame.

He lowered to his knees in front of me so we were eye level.

"What's up with you? Did you and Shay get into it?" Concern etched his handsome features and draped his every word.

I bit the side of my thumb. "I've been uneasy since we got here. I know it sounds crazy, but I'm pretty sure someone is watching me. It's weird."

"It's not." He tugged on my ponytail and regarded me with expectancy.

"I keep hearing unexplainable noises. I was freaked out, so I haven't slept here all week. If I'm honest, this is the first time I've felt safe since we arrived."

"Good, because ain't nothing gonna happen with me around."

He winked at me and pulled his plain tee over his head. I swallowed hard. I'd seen his body many times—both in person and online—but I doubted I would ever get used to it. He made his pecs jump before he left the bedroom.

Somehow, I fell asleep while Nick showered but was awakened when his rough hands tugged on my boy shorts.

"Let me taste you, Keke. Please."

I melted. I couldn't take my eyes off him. Freak Nick was my man, and he wanted to—scratch that, he begged to eat my pussy. I was on the verge of an orgasm already.

"Tell me I can taste our pussy, baby."

"Yes, Nick. Do as you please."

His eyes flashed with an emotion I couldn't identify. Maybe lust or sexual frustration doused with desire. He was naked except for his designer briefs. I'd teased him about those *Hood Body Briefs* until he told me the origin story of the creator.

Malik Malone was a driven young black man who went from delivering pleasure packages for Glamazon to owning his own business. I made a mental note to hit him up on Instabook and thank him for his product. I didn't think there was a garment that could make Nick more enticing, but those briefs were top tier. I was mesmerized by the way they fit his toned thighs and rested against the V shape at his hips.

Nick scooted me to the edge of the bed and face planted between my legs. He licked my yoni like I was a popsicle on a humid summer day. It was the eye contact that made me want to unravel. He reached up and rolled my nipple between his fingers.

"Nick," I moaned.

He continued without a verbal response. The only sounds between us were his slurps and sips of my juices.

"I wish you would ride my face. Just pull my head down there, and I'll eat your pussy any day of the week."

Those words from his mouth—between pauses from giving me the best head I ever had—was enough to cause the eruption that made me bend then arch my back. My body quaked uncontrollably, and Nick was turned on because I hadn't let his head go. I tried but failed as my body convulsed.

He stood and stepped out of his briefs. I'd nearly missed him rolling the condom on because my body was preoccupied with the aftershocks of an oral induced orgasm.

"I need to be inside of you, Girlfriend Keke."

He joined me on top of the bed and glided inside of me in one fell swoop.

My knees quaked.

"I've been crazy without you."

Nick rolled his hips, and I took it as my sign to let loose. I spread my legs until they rested on either side of him, putting me in a split. Years of dancing prepared me for this moment.

"Got damn, girl."

Nick talked shit, but he stayed in my pussy so long I doubted it affected him like he said. We moved from the bed to the wall and ended up with him seated on a chair positioned in front of the mirror. I slid my legs through the spaces on the sides of the chair and rode that man like I had bills to pay.

His large hands gripped my ass while I bounced and grinded in his lap. Nick took the opportunity to lift my shirt and feast on my breasts. I'd had a complex about them until he entered my life. No matter how small they were, he sucked and handled them like they were double Ds.

I took it upon myself to lean in and mark him the way he'd done me. Nick wasn't light skinned, but he was bright enough that the passion mark would be easily visible.

"You claiming me, baby?"

I nodded.

"You so fuckin' sexy, girl."

He slapped my ass, and my body responded. I didn't have as much experience as Nick, but I'd had a few decent lovers in the past. Multiple orgasms weren't completely foreign, but it also hadn't been common for me. Yet, my perfect lap dance morphed into a messy, rhythmless grind as another one tore through me.

"Nick," I moaned next to his ear.

"Yeah, baby."

My body bucked. My chest caved as if I'd been punched. And my body shook like a leaf. He stopped his forceful movements and barely rocked his hips while he smoothed back the hair in my face.

"I have never seen somebody look so pretty when they cum."

I giggled, and the action resulted in a Kegel around Nick's dick. His eyes drifted closed.

"Can I fuck you in front of this mirror, baby?"

I hummed in the affirmative. He helped me up and turned me to face the mirror, entering me from behind. Nick slapped my ass cheeks again and gawked at me through the mirror.

"I'll eat your pussy and give you good dick every day if you let me."

At this point, I was afraid I would die if I had another orgasm. I squeezed my eyes shut in the hopes that his words wouldn't take me there.

"Open your eyes, baby," he pleaded.

I did. Nick's beautiful, tattoo free body rocked in and out of me. His stamina was unmatched. There was a vast difference between my video game playing ex and this international athlete. I looked back at him, and his knees buckled.

I leaned down to touch the floor and bounced my ass against his pelvis.

"Fuck, Keke. I'm about to nut."

His strokes got deeper, but I was here for all of it. I met those strokes with equal shakes, doing my best to return the pleasure he'd given me.

"Give it to me, Freak Nick."

He sucked in a breath. The next thing I knew, he'd pulled out of me, snatched off the condom, and released his seed across my bare ass cheeks. I came again.

Nick

I shot up from the bed when she shrieked.

"What's wrong?"

Her eyes were wide as she peered toward the door. "Somebody's in here."

"Baby, Shayla is in here."

Keke shook her head. "Shay won't get up until late afternoon. It's three a.m."

I was gone off this girl, because all I wanted to do was sleep. But by the look on her face, I wouldn't be able to get her back in my arms until I walked through her suite to reassure her we were alone.

Her eyes shifted from the door to my hard dick. "It's your fault. You've been rubbing your soft ass against me all night."

I was able to pull my briefs and shorts over my erection but decided I wouldn't waste time with a shirt. If someone was in the suite, they would catch a fade, and I would once again be knee deep in Kiara's pussy.

With a smirk on my face, I slowly opened the door. I couldn't decide if I was spooked out because I'd never been to the Midnight Sands Resort or if Keke's fearful energy had affected me, but I was convinced someone was inside too. I backed into the room and fumbled in my bag until I found my pistol.

Kiara sucked in a breath but said nothing. I hoped she wouldn't give me shit about it. I moved back to the door and slowly peered around the darkened suite. As I made my way to the middle point between Kiara's side and Shay's, rustling sounds from outside the door caught my attention. I opened the door and stepped out but saw nothing.

"Come back in, Nick," Kiara's soft voice demanded. She would fuck around and get me killed. I was instantly distracted by the short silk robe she draped over her immaculate body.

I relented because I didn't want her near the door.

"Let's go back to bed," she insisted. "Whoever it is, I'm sure you scared them away."

I wasn't convinced. For now, I would drop the subject, but as soon as we woke up the next morning, I would have to visit the front office to inquire about security footage.

Kiara and Shay opted to stay inside the next night. They said they were tired of the bar, but most likely, they were still creeped out by our uninvited visitor. The security camera positioned near this suite showed a man in a hoodie looking through the windows. There was a guard on foot who was assigned to our suite until we checked out in two days, but we were still unsettled.

Who the hell was that man? Was he there for my girl? I wouldn't hesitate to break a man's jaw over Keke. The staff echoed Kiara's sentiment that the person probably moved along since she wasn't alone. What if I hadn't come? Would she have been safe?

We played dominoes to keep our minds busy, and Keke's uncouth ass wouldn't let us forget how she'd won every game.

"Gerald Towns taught me how to play bones when I was seven. Y'all couldn't beat me if ya worked as a team."

"Whatever, wench," Shay inserted.

We ordered room service and fell into easy conversation. Kiara's best friend, Shayla, was as shaken as Keke, because although she was great company, I doubted her first choice for her vacation was kicking back with us.

"If you want to go out, we'll go with you," I said to Shay as she returned her plate to the service cart.

"I'm good, but thanks for the offer."

Kiara cuddled next to me then flipped the channel to a show I'd never seen.

"I knew he wasn't shit?" I asked with my brows practically touching my hairline.

"Here you go with this. I told you not to watch this show with him," Shay said as she headed toward her side of the suite.

"Don't leave now. What is this?" I called after Shay. She shook her head and released a belly laugh, closing the door behind her.

"Is she really good?" I asked Kiara.

Her head bounced up and down, and she had a silly grin on her face. "She's been caking with this dude named Sean. The show gave her a reason to stay in and talk to him, which is what she wanted to do anyway. Shay acts like she's never going to settle down, but she likes this guy."

The show started, and Keke's attention was locked on the screen.

"Baby, what the hell is this?"

"Guests, and sometimes their friends, test their man to see if he's cheating."

I sighed. "This is entrapment."

She muted the show and turned to look up at me. "If a woman with a fat ass and big perky breasts hit on you and you knew I wouldn't find out, would you take her number?"

"I didn't say all that. I saw what happened when I didn't punt Sierra and announce to the school I had a girlfriend named Keke. You think I'd give a big titty woman my number?"

She giggled. "I asked would you take her number, silly man."

"Same thing, and no, I would not."

She leaned up and pressed her soft lips on mine. My dick sprang to attention like the whipped puppy it was, earning me another giggle from Keke. She unmuted the TV and gasped.

"What's wrong, baby?" I was on high alert.

She pointed at the screen. "It's Quincy."

"Who?" The man looked familiar. Had she fucked this dude? If she was pressed over another man she used to fool around with, who was now on a TV show about cheating, I was about to flip.

"Coach Malcolm."

Since when did she get on a first name basis with this fool?

The episode was bizarre as hell. Apparently, men could call the show and have their ladies followed like women did. Coach's girl wasn't cheating. She respectfully turned down the guy they used to pretend to hit on her. She was attractive and well-spoken. And for whatever reason, she was into Coach Quincy Malcolm.

It was Quincy who was off. He wanted the host to do some wild stuff even the show wasn't comfortable with. They had a formula on how they exposed their guests, but Quincy asked them to delve deeper into her privacy. In the end, Coach Malcolm decided he didn't want to tell her she'd been set up, in hopes that he could save his relationship, but what if she saw the episode? What if one of her coworkers or family members sent it to her? This shit was full of red flags.

"Let's watch something else," Kiara said quietly. "This creeper energy is freaking me out."

I pulled her close. "You're safe with me."

She leaned up and pressed her lips to mine. I would be damned if I didn't cash in another round, given the freedom from children and small ass Saint Des. I'd deepened the kiss and was ready to go. Kiara moaned into my mouth, matching my energy. Before we could make it back to her room, my phone rang. She backed away from me.

"Take it. We have time."

I groaned and snatched the phone from my shorts. "What?"

She smirked and created space between us.

"Is this how you speak to your future employer?" my coach asked.

"Coach Freeman, my apologies. I'm on vacation until Saturday."

"Retirement looks good on you, Young. There's a week-long training coming up at the end of the month. I need you here. It lays out exactly what's expected of an agent and how to go about getting certified if you choose to do so. You're popular enough that it's not mandatory, but the certification could positively affect your income."

"Do I need to take the certification overseas? How many weeks is it?" My eyes were on Kiara as she mindlessly scrolled social media. I didn't want to be away from her for more than a few days. Historically, I wasn't a relationship type of man, but I moved differently when it came to her.

"The certification program is online, but the training is in person."

"Send me the details."

"Already done. And Nick?"

"Yes, Coach?"

"Bring her with you."

I laughed. I'd forgotten the Darkhaven suits tracked our social media accounts. He knew about Kiara. Maybe he'd only seen her feet, but I'd never posted anything remotely close to a relationship before. Beautiful women, absolutely. Girlfriends, never.

I disconnected the call and contemplated how much I should share about my uncertain future. Would she have an opinion? Would she go with me?

"I've heard about this," she said as she returned to the couch where I stood. We were on our way to the room until my cock-blocking ass coach called.

I sat down because I wanted to be up under her, whether we were fucking or not. "Heard about what?"

"Men in the military who have a hard time transitioning to civilian life."

"I ain't in the military, girl."

"Hasn't being a professional athlete been your entire identity from like age ten until now?"

I nodded hesitantly.

"That's like twenty years. Somehow, you're supposed to know what you want to do with the rest of your life."

I hadn't considered it from her perspective. "Come with me to this training."

"What training? When? I have a dance studio and a kid to look after," she responded with wide eyes.

"Close it. You need a break, and I know Kace spends time with his dad over the summer. Come with me."

She bit her bottom lip, and I was instantly jealous of her teeth.

"Help me figure out if this agent shit is a good look."

"Agent?"

I talked her ears off about possibly working with the Darkhavens and the job Cyrus's uncle Mitch offered me at *Fine and Fitbody Bootcamp*. I assured her I'd live in Saint Des either way, but the agent job would require travel. Kiara insisted I was in a win-win situation, and if I was worried about money working at Mitch's gym, I could put that to bed. She said the type of women who worked out there would keep plenty of money in my pockets, solely because of the way I looked. If I got those women into the shape like she assumed I could, the memberships would multiply.

We never made it to her room. We watched a movie and fell asleep on the couch, fully clothed. I loved every moment of it.

CHAPTER 13

Kiara

Our last day at the Midnight Sands Resort and Spa was absolutely embarrassing. Nick said he would meet Shay and me at the beach after his workout. We sat near the shoreline where the palm trees sagged, almost dipping their leaves into the teal water. I rested against my lounge chair comfortably. The huge umbrella shielded us from the beautiful yet unforgiving sun.

She and I were chatting about any and everything when he finally made his way outside. I'd seen Nick naked countless times, but his sculpted body in those trunks did something to me. I spilled my drink and almost fell flat on my face trying to get to him, but luckily, Shay grabbed my arm. She laughed the whole time, but she wouldn't let me make a complete fool of myself.

Women and men alike stared at his assured gate, whispering about who he was. Nick Young had the confidence of a celebrity. Some of the men correctly pegged him as an athlete, only they'd labeled him a football player who probably didn't get playing time. Jealousy wasn't a good look on them. But I'd take envy over the thirst radiating off groups of women who were also on girls' trips looking for trouble.

The moment he laid eyes on me, the corners of his lips lifted. He'd seen the stares and waved them off. This wasn't new to him, but it was to me. I fidgeted with my ponytail and coverup. If God was who he said, maybe Nick hadn't seen me trip like a lovesick sorority girl.

"Hey," I said, peering up at his mostly covered face. His sunglasses were simple but had somehow made him more attractive.

He didn't respond, just wrapped large hands around my hips and dipped his head to kiss me.

"Ugh, y'all make me sick," Shay said.

"You can join in if you want," Nick teased.

"What?" Shay and I said in unison. I slapped his arm as he laughed.

"You're best friends. What could go wrong?" Sarcasm laced his words.

"You're not my type, Freak Nick," Shay shot back.

"I'm everybody's type."

Shay reclaimed her beach chair. "You're not *my* kind of freak."

"Don't mind Shay. She wants an unhinged man to clap her cheeks in broad daylight."

Nick settled beside me with a deep scowl on his painfully handsome face. "We did that."

Panic washed over me. Shay and I were close, and we joked around, but she didn't need to know the details of our sex life.

"Did what?" she asked, closing the book her eyes had been glued to all day.

"I clapped Keke's cheeks in her driveway. She didn't tell you?" he asked matter-of-factly.

Nick was fine. But maybe his social media description wasn't completely accurate. To most, he was a few chili peppers on a scale from zero to five. But with me, I was heated thinking about it.

"Umm," I stammered.

"Save it. I don't want to hear all the filthy footnotes. That's what this is for." She held up her book. I laughed, but Nick's brows furrowed once more. I dodged a bullet with that story. Poor Darian.

<hr>

We didn't stay much longer, as I told them both I had a weird feeling again. *Someone was watching me, but who?* Since Nick had seen the footage of the strange man outside of our suite and told us about it, they trusted my gut, and we got out of there. I didn't regret our trip, but I would likely never return to the resort. Too many unsettling feelings.

If I wasn't already crazy about Nick, my infatuation tripled when I discovered he'd purchased a one-way ticket to see me. When we got to the ticket counter, he announced how he needed a seat next to me and that he didn't give a damn how much it would cost.

"That's real cute, sir, but it doesn't work like that. We have limited seats available. You can purchase one of them and swap seats once you're on the aircraft until your heart's content."

Shay guffawed. She changed her tune when he presented her with three first class seats.

"Thank you," she said while bouncing her shoulders. "We not in the same row though, right? I don't want to see none of y'all PG-13 freaky deaky antics."

He did put her in a different row, but once again surprised me when all we did was talk. I had my bare feet on him at his request, but otherwise, we rested peacefully.

Halfway into our flight, I broke the silence. "I want to ask a dumb question," I said barely above a whisper.

"Impossible. What's up?" His eyes were closed, but his hands massaged my feet. I was seated facing the aisle with my legs in his lap.

"How did you really get the name?"

His eyes fluttered open and gazed at me thoughtfully. "Why you ask?"

I shrugged. "I should know if I'm going to be Mrs. Freak Nick."

He leaned in and pecked my lips. "The real story or the fake one?"

"Both."

He recounted how his dad swiped his mom from her ex-boyfriend at Freaknik and how there was a good chance it was where he was conceived. His parents admitted they were pregnant with him before they got married, but they wouldn't confirm the location of his conception. Nick said in his heart he knew he was the result of the epic spring break festival. He told me about Cyrus and how it ended up as his line name for their fraternity and consequently his handle on social media.

I beamed up at him. His honesty made me emotionally secure. I never had safety with Darian, and he was the only reference I had for an authentic relationship.

"I still love women—but I don't need a gang of them to be satisfied. You wanna know something else?"

I nodded, hanging on to his every word.

"I've never juggled a bunch of women at once. Too much of a headache. But I don't bother correcting people's assumptions. I guess I'm trying to say it's not much of a leap for me to kick it with only you. It's a relief."

My mouth fell open. He licked his lips.

"You look sexy as hell." He angled his head, cracking his neck.

Nick rested his hand between my open legs. "Just like I thought. It's warm as fuck down here."

The stewardess conveniently found herself pressed against my man's shoulder. When her eyes landed on me, she scowled.

"We're about to land. You need to fasten your seat belt," she barked, then she continued through first class collecting trash.

"I guess she told you," Nick teased.

Bitter flight attendant aside, I was on cloud nine. Freak Nick wanted to be settled… with me.

<hr>

When we returned to Saint Des, my shoulders relaxed. Our flight was smooth save for the busy body attendant. I was thankful for the time to wrap my head around all that awaited me once we touched down. I'd have to get back to my girls at the studio and my mommy duties, but at least I was rested. It was the reason Shay and I planned these annual getaways.

Shay declined Nick's offer to give her a ride home and instead opted to call a rideshare. We both had each other's location. I got text notifications of her driver and when she arrived at her destination. I couldn't blame her. Nick couldn't keep his hands off me. Shay was happy for us but not up for being a third wheel any longer.

His fingers intertwined in a belt loop of my jeans, which seemed nearly impossible with his bag on his back and my stacked bag combo being rolled with his other hand. He refused to let me carry my belongings despite me reminding him I got them here fine.

"I got this. When you gon' let me eat you again?"

He wasn't talking about food. The airport was full of people, some of whom could hear him.

"Nick." I'd never been a fan of PDA, but this banter was a

whole other level. I peeked around, and an older woman with a head full of gray hair blushed as she walked slowly beside us.

"I don't give a damn about these people. Show me one woman who wouldn't want her man eating her pussy every day."

I slapped his arm, but the older woman piped up.

"My George, rest his soul, said it was one of his favorite pastimes."

"See," Nick teased. "Give me some," he said to her with a high five she willingly returned.

I waved goodbye and hoped her kids checked on her often. I was in my head about it until Nick broke into my thoughts. "Want me to ask her to lunch?"

My head flew in his direction. "Huh?"

"She was nice. And she let her old man, George, eat her pussy like he asked. Maybe she could talk some sense into you."

I laughed. "You'd do that?"

"Yeah, why not?"

I misjudged him. He was such a kind soul. It almost didn't match up to what he looked like on the outside. I needed to thank his mother for the job she did with Nick Young.

We walked in silence through the parking lot. I wasn't as open or giving as he was. I didn't know that lady or who her family was, so I didn't take him up on his offer to invite her to lunch. Maybe I could learn a thing or two from him. My phone rang, and my mood instantly shifted.

"Hi, son."

"Hey, Mama. Are you back yet?"

"I just got here. Is everything OK?"

"Yes. I wanted to make sure you got home safe. Talk to you later."

He hung up, and I stood there in shock.

Nick loaded the car. "How's Kace of base?"

"He's good. He asked if I was home safe."

"My man. That's good."

I sighed. It was good. He'd grown in such a short amount of time. I wouldn't fight it. I would take it all in.

"Not this shit again."

I blinked myself from my introspection at the sound of Nick's frustration in time to see another one of his tires was slashed.

The police didn't do shit. They had the nerve to criticize me for my choice of parking and suggested I get a new car. After I mentally recorded their badge numbers, I dared them to make another disrespectful comment. Kiara helped mediate the situation, and since they liked her, they agreed to stay on the lookout for any questionable activity between our residences. When she mentioned the bizarre encounter we had on our vacation, their ears perked up. One of them jotted the information in his tiling notebook.

They left us in the uncovered airport parking lot to fend for ourselves. It was fine by me. The one with the belly had one more time to stare at my girl's ass. He was begging to catch these hands.

I was elbow deep in changing another tire. Kiara was seated on her suitcase, squirming around. Her freaky ass was turned on by menial tasks like these.

"I can smell you through your pants."

She sucked in a breath.

"Why you all worked up?"

"Have you seen yourself?"

I threw my head back and laughed. "I got it like that."

She nodded.

"Seriously though. I know you already surprised me on my vacation and spent time with me. I'm not trying to be clingy…"

"Spit it out, girlfriend."

"Will you stay with me tonight? Until I can figure out a more permanent situation. I'm nervous to be at the house by myself."

I dropped the lug wrench and wiped my hands on a towel I kept in the car with my tools. "Come here."

She stood and melted into me.

"I got you. Don't worry. I got you."

Kiara

When Kace made it home on Sunday, Nick was still there. In a move that surprised me: I'd given him a key. He wanted to keep an eye on his sister, and with all the errands I ran, I wasn't always available to let him in when he made it to my house. I told Kace he'd be around more, but he didn't seem bothered at all. Nick was asleep on the couch. I learned he took naps daily. It was the cutest thing to see a man as big as him rest like a baby.

"I don't even have practice until tomorrow," Kace fussed. He brushed past me.

"You know you don't do well in the morning, and now that school is out, Coach moved your practices to what you call the buttcrack of dawn."

Kace huffed. "I'll do it in the morning."

"And when you leave your glove or your cleats, I'm not driving you back here to get it."

"OK."

Kace must have raised his voice because we both jumped when Nick asked, "What's the problem?"

I forgot he was here. This was our normal dynamic. If Darian stepped in, it usually escalated. I had no idea how Nick would respond and if Kace would be receptive. Kace opened his mouth, but I interjected.

"I'm trying to get Kace to prep for practice in the morning."

"Why?" Nick asked. Kace's smirk deepened, and I reared my head back in disbelief.

I wanted to say because I said so but figured it wouldn't help the situation. "His practice starts at eight tomorrow morning." I reiterated I wouldn't be driving home if Kace forgot something.

"Don't."

"But he won't be able to play if he's late for practice or if he isn't prepared."

"So."

I swear I wanted to slap this beautiful, frustrating man upside his well-groomed head. "So?"

Nick entered the kitchen fully. His physical presence was intimidating, but his words were gentle. "If he can't play, that's on him. Don't save him from his rock bottom."

I huffed, becoming increasingly aware of why my son made this sound when he was irritated.

"Kace, you wanna play baseball?"

"Yeah. I mean yes."

Nick opened his hands like the problem was solved.

"If you forget your gear, who's fault is it if you can't suit up?" Nick asked with a tad more authority in his voice.

"Mine." Kace weighed Nick's words like it never dawned on him it was his responsibility.

"Go get everything you need for practice tomorrow," Nick ordered.

Kace scurried from the room like he did when Coach Malcolm barked commands to the team. Nick winked at me but said nothing.

"What are you doing?" I asked.

"You trust me?"

Our pattern of answering a question with a question was only fun when I did the dodging. I stomped my foot.

"I'll take that as a sort of."

Kace bumbled back into the kitchen with his baseball backpack on and hat in his hand.

"Is this everything?" Nick asked.

Kace nodded.

Nick took the bag from him and walked into the living room, with both Kace and I on his heels. He sat on the couch and dumped the bag out, spilling the contents across the floor.

"Pack your bag."

Kace's shoulders sank, but he did as he was told. Within a minute or so, Kace had his bag repacked with a huge smile on his face. Nick took the bag from him, unzipped it, and dumped it again. These were the types of lessons mothers were ill-equipped to teach. I prayed he wouldn't take it too far though.

Kace repacked the bag. This time, he threw the stuff inside. When I tried to say something, Nick held up his hand to stop me. I didn't know whether to cuss him out or take him in the next room to bust it open.

He presented the bag to Nick, and once again, Nick opened his bag and tossed his glove, helmet, cleats, and water bottle across the floor.

"Pack your bag, Kace."

Kace kissed his teeth. "You is not my dad," he roared.

Kace stood, but he hadn't left the room.

"I know that. We all know I'm not your dad. But what does that have to do with your mom having to beg you to pack your own bag? It's not her responsibility to pack your shit. It's her job to make sure she drives you there until you can. It's her job to make your food until you learn how to do it yourself. But it is not her job to make sure you're on time and prepared."

Kace paced the living room. He hadn't stormed out.

"You know I played at a professional level?"

"Everybody knows that."

"I didn't get there with somebody holding my hand. My mom didn't make me shoot around every morning before school. She sure as hell didn't make sure I had my basketball shoes. If I forgot to tell her practice was moved up thirty minutes and we got there late, whose fault was it?"

"But you couldn't drive."

"That's why it was my job to tell her when I needed to be there, and to remind her fifty times if I needed to. I told her more than once when I wanted a new game."

My baby boy smiled. He actually cracked a smile.

"Are you any good?" Nick pressed.

"I'm the best on the team, ain't I, Mama?"

I nodded because he was.

"All the more reason not to let your team down. You're supposed to be the first one there and the last to leave each night."

"Is that what you did?"

Nick nodded. "Now pack your bag, superstar."

He did as he was told. Kace packed his bag again with a renewed sense of urgency. My chest swelled. While I may not have directly doled out this mini teach, I would take credit for laying the foundation. When Kace had his items repacked in his book bag, Nick took it and placed his hands on the zipper.

"Do I need to do it again?"

"No!" Kace shouted.

"Good. Take your bag back to your room and make sure you're ready to go at seven fifteen tomorrow."

My eyes widened.

"Do you have an alarm clock?"

Kace stole a glance at me.

"Kiara is your alarm clock?" he asked. Once again, I wanted to shout that he was only eleven, but I bit my cheek to remain quiet.

"I have one. I just don't use it," he admitted.

"Set your alarm clock and be ready on time."

Kace nodded and bopped out of the room.

"What was that?" I asked once we were alone.

"Respect and accountability. It's going to make your life easier, but it's gonna cost you the baby boy you're holding onto."

"I don't even want to know what that means."

I was in such a good mood—the last thing I wanted was Nick to resume the instructor role again. I'd had more than enough schooling for today. Besides, Kace would be my baby boy until he left this earth.

He followed me back into the kitchen. "Make me something to eat. I'm hungry as hell," he announced as he slapped my ass.

I rolled my eyes because, somehow, the two had ganged up on me. Not only did I have to keep quiet to avoid behaving disrespectfully, but I was also responsible for feeding these athletes.

I pulled out the spaghetti Kace and I had eaten for lunch.

"Is this what you feeding this boy?" Nick asked, laughing.

I crossed my arms and popped my hip. I'd had enough. If they wanted different food, they could put their heads together and make it themselves.

"Yep," Kace said as he bopped back into the kitchen to grab an apple from the fridge.

I slammed the Tupperware on the counter and turned to leave until I could calm myself but was pulled back by strong arms.

"I'm not criticizing you. I'm sure it's amazing, but it's not enough. I guarantee you he's still hungry. That's probably why he has an attitude all the time."

"Yes!" Kace exclaimed.

Nick grabbed him by the sleeve of his shirt. "Here." He opened and closed the cabinets until he found a jar of peanut butter. This beautiful frustrating man asked me for a knife then sliced what was left of Kace's apple. He dropped a large spoonful of the peanut butter and placed it on a plate with the fruit.

"It's more protein. It'll hold him over for about an hour," Nick said, handing the plate to Kace.

"Thanks, Nick."

Nick gave him a nod then steadied his gaze on me. "I like him."

I shrugged. "I didn't invite you over to join forces with my son and gang up on me."

"That's not what I'm doing."

He tugged on my waist until I was flushed against him. "You mad now?"

I shook my head and pulled my lip between my teeth. "The opposite actually."

He pressed his lips against mine softly but pulled back before we got carried away. "Damn, girlfriend." His gaze lifted in the direction of Kace who ate his snack in the living room. "Later."

"OK." With the way this man's scent surrounded my body and lingered in my nose, I would agree to anything.

"Now heat up my food, woman."

He waltzed out of the kitchen and joined Kace.

Ain't this some shit. I giggled to myself and did as I was told.

CHAPTER 14

Nick

The flight to Cortavia was as long as it always was. I'd been able to sleep for most of it because I fucked Kiara until neither of us could stand before I left. She stayed home, opting not to do the week with me. She had obligations to her dance studio and didn't want to lose herself in our new relationship.

I respected her stance. In fact, it made me want her more. We spent most of our time together since I didn't have anything full time, and Jackie and the kids needed me less and less. It was essential for them to bond without my interference. Jack assured me the three of them living in my home without me there all the time was a blessing. She could focus on being a parent without the stress of bills or school since it was summer.

As the driver navigated us from the Cortavia International Airport to the Darkhaven's gymnasium, the same questions bounced around in my mind. What was next for me? Was I moving too fast with Kiara? Was she the reason I was neutral about the prospect of being an agent?

There was also the opportunity with *Fine and Fitbody Bootcamp* with Uncle Mitch. I loved my dad. Our close relationship was why I found strong male role models in every stage of my life. Uncle Mitch was an OG who I was excited to spend more time with. I'd scheduled a sit-down with him for after I returned to the States to weigh my options.

I wore a knee-length winter coat and Timberland boots that were both powerless against the frigid chill in the air. I'd overdone it with my gear. Saint Des huddled around a nice eighty degrees during the summer in contrast to Cortavia's sixty-one degrees.

The residents were unbothered by the breezy temperature common for the coldest country on this side of the world. They wore long sleeves and shorts. When I was here last, the weather was of no consequence. I made double what my peers made because of my skill and the undesirable location.

Besides, black people were everywhere despite what the media portrayed back home. There was a group of West Africans who lived in Cortavia for two generations. I'd dated a few of them and had no complaints. A girl I used to kick it with hit me up after she saw I posted Kiara.

She'd gotten the impression I would reach out to her when I was ready to settle down. I left her message on read. She was fine but couldn't hold a candle to Kiara Towns. My meat got hard thinking about Keke. I had it bad.

I navigated to my photos and gawked at pictures of her from the Midnight Sands Resort and Spa. My mind raced as I regarded her. I'd loved my time here as a ball player, but at the sight of the dark meat peeking out beneath the tiny shorts she wore, I had an attitude because I couldn't get to her.

We pulled up to the hotel where the other agents would stay. My stomach fluttered, and I was jittery. Either I'd spent too much time with her squirrely ass to assume she needed me, or something was wrong. While the hotel porter helped me with my bag, I called Kiara. It was daytime here but evening in Saint Des.

"Hey." She was preoccupied. If I was an insecure man, I might have been concerned.

"I miss you." I hadn't tried to downplay my thoughts. It was the truth, and I wanted her to know.

"You just left." Kiara laughed, but it was forced.

"You at your house? What's wrong?"

"The power went out. It's been storming, but it's weird that my lights were affected because I can see the neighbors still have theirs on."

I couldn't keep her safe here, and my frustration grew from a flicker to an inferno.

"I have a flashlight. I'm going to check the circuit breaker instead of sitting in here scared."

"Where is it?"

"On the side of my house. This isn't my first year renting this house. I've done it before."

"Don't go outside." My voice was more demanding than I intended. I wasn't flustered with her. I was irritated by the entire situation. "Is Kace with you?"

"No, dad. He's with his grandmother. My father is literally the only person who can boss me like this."

I smirked.

"Sir, you're all set," the receptionist said in a thick accent.

I gave her a nod but said nothing. "Can you take this up to my room?" I asked the hotel porter who immediately whisked my belongings in the opposite direction.

"OK, big time. You're still famous over there, Nick Young."

"I'm famous everywhere," I teased. She tried to lighten the mood but hadn't succeeded. Her door opened.

"Kiara, don't go outside. Close the door."

She did as I asked with a huff. My shoulders sagged when the lock clicked, alerting me she was once again safe inside.

"I'll send my dad over."

"You don't have to—"

"The neighbors' lights are on, and you're the only house without power. Let me call you back when he's on the way."

She was quiet. I pulled the phone from my face to see the call hadn't disconnected.

"Please," I added for good measure.

"Fine."

"Thank you. I'll call you back."

I navigated to my contacts and dialed my dad's number.

"You were here a minute ago. I know you are not calling to tell me you miss me and your mama at five dollars an hour."

"I need your help."

He cleared his throat and moved from where I assumed he and my mom were settled for the night.

"OK. What's going on?"

"Can you drive past Kiara's house?"

"Who?" There was a hint of amusement in his voice.

"I wanted you to meet her at dinner when I get back, but her power is out. Nobody else in her neighborhood is having the same issue."

"I'm not hearing the problem, son. I'm sure you can walk her through it."

"The breaker is on the outside of her house. Somebody slashed my tire in her driveway a little while back."

"What?"

"It happened again at the airport when I surprised her by showing up to her girls' trip. And before you ask, we called the police both times."

"Send me the address."

I shared it via text message. "I did. Can you call me when you get there?"

"I know what I'm doing."

My dad disconnected our call. As tense as I was, his attitude was surprisingly refreshing. I paced the lobby and eventually marched up to my room feeling powerless. I prayed my dad would figure out what the hell was up with Kiara's house.

Kiara

Nick texted and gave me a heads up his dad was en route to my house. I wanted to sneak out and flip the switch myself, then his father wouldn't have to go to any trouble. I could've called my own dad if I'd been thinking straight, but Nick was determined to handle it his own way. The fact that he was in another country worried about me was the reason I had a goofy grin on my face—even if it was an overreaction. Maybe I didn't hate men.

Light knocks sounded at my door.

"Hello, Mr. Young. I'm Kiara. I'm really sorry you had to go out of your way."

"Nice to meet you, Kiara. You're Gerald Town's daughter?"

I nodded.

Jerry Young was a handsome man. Nick didn't resemble him, but their mannerisms were practically identical. He responded with a nod and a grunt. It didn't bother me that he was a man of few words; I only hoped he wouldn't hold it against me that he was out at this time of night on my account.

The rain had slowed. His raincoat was almost as imposing as his large frame. Jerry refused to come in and instead stood silently.

"Umm, OK. The breaker box is on the left of my house, opposite the garage."

He nodded. I handed him a flashlight, then he disappeared into the darkness. *Yikes.*

"Did he get it back on?" Nick asked the moment he answered my call.

"He's working on it. I should've called my own dad. He didn't say much to me."

"What are you wearing?"

I looked down at myself. "It's not that bad."

"Yeah right. Don't take it personal. My mom is the one with all the personality and home training."

The lights reappeared, and my television came to life. Jerry knocked at the door and opened his mouth to speak.

"It's your dad," I said.

"Put me on speaker."

I did as he asked.

"Everything OK?" Nick asked. I liked his bossy side, but now wasn't the time to acknowledge it.

"It was turned off," his dad said. "Whoever did it didn't bother trying to hide it. Deep, muddy footsteps were tracked from the side of the house to the street where I'm assuming they parked. Good thing Nick told you not to go outside. It looks like they were waiting for you to come out alone."

It was the most he'd spoken since he'd arrived.

"The hell?" Nick boomed through the phone.

"I'll make sure to circle the block a few times before I go home, but whoever it was left because of me," Jerry continued.

"I'm calling the police. Do you still have their card, Keke?" Nick asked.

"Yes."

"I'm going to head out. Stay safe," his dad said with a small wave.

"Thank you for stopping by, Mr. Young."

He nodded and left.

Once he was gone, panic set in. The eerie feeling I had at the resort wasn't here when the power went out, but it was back now. What would've happened had Nick not called to check on me?

Nick

"I'm coming home tomorrow."

"I can't let you do that. I'll be fine. Like I said, I can call my own dad." Kiara sighed.

My concentration would be split the entire week. There wasn't a chance in hell I would stay in Cortavia while someone meant Kiara harm.

"I'm your man, right?"

"Yes."

No disclaimers and no explanations from her, just the magical word.

"Then trust me. I'll attend the first day. As soon as it's done, I'm coming home to you."

"OK."

"One more thing."

"What is it?"

"Do you and Shay still do sleepovers? I mean, I know you a grown ass woman."

"If I ask her, she'll come."

"Good. Call her when we hang up."

"OK." She was frustrated with me, but it was a relief she didn't fight me on any of my demands.

"Kiara," I hummed.

"Yes, Nick."

"I need some pussy." I sat in an oversized chair next to a wall-sized window facing a lush green mountain landscape untouched by man. Now that Kiara's safety was somewhat taken care of, I missed her body. If she was here, we wouldn't leave my suite for shit.

I hadn't unpacked, and now I had no plans of getting comfortable. I would attend day one of the training this afternoon then fly out tomorrow.

"Come get some," she purred.

Her matching my energy was motivation to handle business and return to Saint Des. Fuck this job.

Kiara

"Thanks for coming last night," I said to Shay as I slid her a plate and a cup of coffee. After I texted her what happened, she came over like the rider she was.

"You owe me. Quincy has the best head I've ever had in my life."

My eyes bulged, and I stopped in front of her.

"Don't tell me you and Quincy..."—Shay slouched as her head dropped—"this town is too damn small."

"Quincy Malcolm?" I know good and well my girl hadn't fucked Coach Malcolm.

"Maybe." She scrolled her phone until she found his social media page. "Him?"

"I haven't messed around with him if that's what you were thinking. He's Kace's baseball coach." I covered my mouth but couldn't smother the laugh when she showed me his picture. He was attractive, but he wasn't my type.

Shay shrugged. "Doesn't bother me none."

I continued in the kitchen until I remembered he was on an episode of the show she criticized me for watching.

"Come look at this." There was no way I could blurt it out in a way that would've made sense. She needed to see with her own two eyes.

I used the remote to scroll through the episodes.

"You and Freaky Nick are a couple for real now for him to suffer through this. I'm not watching it. You don't need to either. It's obvious your man hating phase has finally run its course." She knocked into me, and I almost fell. I loved my heavy-handed girl which was why I had to let her see the truth about her sneaky link. I let the episode roll, despite the stink eye she threw my way. Her mouth fell open.

"That's…"

She sat in disbelief.

"I'm not saying you can't date him. I'm saying be careful. Maybe this is old and he's a different man. I couldn't let you proceed without giving you a heads up."

"I like a little crazy like the next woman, but his shit is documented." She scratched her head. "This is wild. Who would've guessed something good would come of this damn show."

We were quiet for several seconds then burst into laughter.

"Are you going to tell him you saw it?"

"Hell no. I'm going to keep this info tucked away and use it if, and when, I need to. I better head out. It's daylight. Your man should be home soon anyway," she teased.

I rolled my eyes and walked her to the door. It was night in Cortavia. Nick wouldn't get back until late this evening. I would be ready when he arrived. He said he wanted some pussy. He didn't have to ask me twice.

Nick

Coach Freeman was pissed when I left early. Ask me if I cared. It wasn't a good fit. Had this opportunity dropped in my life before I met Kiara, I would've been all over it. Add to that, my baby sister needed her big brother, and no amount of money could keep me away.

The training stressed how the agent position would require travel at least five times in a year. Hard pass. I was professional in my delivery of the news to my coach. He assured me the offer didn't have an expiration date—I could revisit it once I was settled with my new lady in Saint Des. Those were his words, not mine.

When I touched down, I headed directly to Kiara's. I sat up the street from her house in my ride for twenty minutes before an unfamiliar car crept by. This boyfriend title had me surveilling her spot like I was the law. I'd spent enough time in her neighborhood to know who did and didn't belong here.

I grabbed my bag and stepped out of my ride. This shit needed to stop already. Once the driver saw me, they turned and peeled out. I couldn't figure out if Kace's dad was capable of this or if one of her other ex's had an issue with me knocking it out the box.

While I had only posted her feet on my page to avoid unnecessary drama toward my lady, Keke uploaded pics of us from her trip. She didn't have as many followers as I did, but she'd made it known to the men who followed her she was taken. Every active territorial impulse in my body eased now that buddy had driven off. And though their absence was a temporary fix to a major concern, my tongue still twitched just thinking about how moving it was that she'd claimed me on the internet.

It was midnight, and Kiara was asleep. It was a good thing she'd given me a key. I let myself in with a smile on my face. I set my bag down and silently prayed Keke slept naked tonight, because I removed my clothes outside of her door. She'd be awakened by some impeccable dick and tongue action. I eased into her room and was both relieved and turned on to be met with a fierce swing of a baseball bat.

It connected with my right bicep before I could announce myself.

"Baby, it's me, with your strong little ass."

The bat dropped to the ground, and when realization crossed her features, she jumped into my arms.

"Oh my God. Nick. You're here."

Her soft bare ass cheeks rested in my hands like they belonged there. She held me tight. And while I couldn't see what she wore, the silk texture of the fabric paired with the succulent flesh pressed against me let me know she was damn near naked.

"Yeah, baby. You're safe."

She pulled back far enough for me to finally kiss her. Our tongues were at war in no time—aggressive in the sense of proving who missed who more. I allowed her to slip down my bare chest which gave me an opportunity to truly take her in. My girl was fine. I could spend a lifetime knee deep in her cheeks.

"Did you wear this for me?"

She nodded and pulled her lip between her teeth. Her eyes raked across my frame like we had all the time in the world. I grabbed her hips and pulled her to the bed so she could straddle me. I wanted my mouth on hers without the need to bend to meet her. I squeezed her cheeks when a moan rumbled deep in her throat.

"Nick," she whined.

I gripped her neck when she wound her hips against me to create friction. I released her and rubbed my rough hands against her back, causing her to arch into me. My hand found her center.

"Damn, Girlfriend Keke. How you this wet already?"

She steadied herself and with ragged breaths said, "Have you seen yourself?"

I smirked then repositioned her so I was on top, and she was beneath me. *Damn, she's future baby mama beautiful.* Her chest rose and fell as she squirmed under my gaze. I wanted to kiss her all over, so that was exactly what I did.

"Please," she moaned. If she wanted me to stop, her salacious whines wouldn't help her case. It was music to my ears.

Her comforter was almost as soft as she was. I licked her neck and nuzzled her breasts, teasing her with nibbles along the way down to our pussy. I positioned her thigh over my shoulder and went to work. Somehow, I'd pretended myself into a legitimate relationship. I didn't know where we were headed yet, but Kiara would be with me from here on out.

Sweet wasn't a strong enough word to describe her essence. Kiara was superior to any candy I'd ever tasted. She was already wet, but putting my mouth on her made her juices intensify. My dick ached to get inside of her. Just when I thought I wouldn't be able to wait any longer, her deep bronze body bucked.

"Nick!" she yelled. She pulled at her bedding and clutched it tightly.

"Yeah, Keke."

Her eyes rolled in the back of her head, and I stood to get a bird's eye view of her pleasure. Her body eventually calmed. I joined her in the disheveled sheets and spread her limp legs to gain entry.

"Let me in, baby," I begged. I'd been with Kiara countless times, and each time, her pussy tightened like it was our first time.

She focused her gaze on me and relaxed. I pushed inside of her and hoped my body could express the deep feelings I had for her, because I didn't have the words. Our groans grew from muted to verbal utterances. I swayed in and out of her unlike any other sexual experience I'd had.

"I love it," she admitted.

"I love you too," was my response. *Fuck.* I hadn't let her fully finish her statement. What she said was she loved *it*. For all I know, she could be in love with my dick and how I made her body quake. Not only was I in my head, but I was also in over my head. I missed Kiara while I was gone. This relationship was mostly brand new. She lifted her upper body and rested on her elbows.

"You love me, Nick?" she asked.

Keke had warmed up to me. No longer did she throw the bitter attitude at me like she did when we first met. She'd agreed when I asked if I was her man, and she relented when I insisted she wait for my dad to check on her when her power went out.

I'd made love to her with my body, and when I got caught up in the moment, the words spilled out. Maybe it was too soon. Maybe I wasn't built for relationships. Maybe I'd avoided love in the past because I was ill-equipped to work through my fears about if things went wrong. Maybe none of that mattered if the relationship was with Keke.

Kiara

He hadn't moved, but his dick pulsed inside of me. My mouth opened. Why I thought I could carry on a conversation with his godzilla sized manhood pleasing me the way only Nick Young could was beyond me. I asked him if he meant it when he said he loved me, but now, neither of us could form words.

"I…I…" he stammered.

I grabbed his face and shoved my tongue inside his mouth. He swayed against me, slow grinding in a manner that screamed more than mere sex.

"I love you… Freak Nick."

He smiled down at me. "I love you, Girlfriend Keke."

He picked up the pace. "Put your feet on my chest."

My body tensed, and tears spilled from my eyes. I'd given up on the possibility I could have another romantic relationship, and *I Knew He Wasn't Shit* hadn't helped. It affirmed my deepest fears about men. I hated them until Nick melted my resolve. Not only was he fine, but he also handled me perfectly. On top of everything, he was a strong role model for my son. Now he fixed his tantalizing, filthy lips to say he loved me.

My body bucked. "Nick!"

He repositioned my jelly-like legs and placed them on his chest then pulled my toes into his mouth. Between licks, he said, "I want you to meet my mom."

Could he be any sexier?

"I want to introduce you to my family."

"Why don't you make me." I loved him and his dick, but this slow grind would take me out if he kept it up. I wanted to be fucked by the man I loved, and by the look in his eyes, he wouldn't have any trouble delivering.

He plunged into me. "What are you trying to do to me, Keke?"

"Get you to fuck me."

His eyes rolled to the back of his head. When they popped open, he wrapped my legs around his waist and stood. He bumped into my end table and backed me against the wall, slamming into me in the most delicious way. His hands gripped my ass and pulled me against him forcefully. Only my back connected to the wall. I had complete trust in Nick. If he let go of me, I would bust my ass. At that moment, I couldn't care less.

CHAPTER 15

Nick

I'd almost pulled a muscle when I fucked Kiara all over her house. I had it so bad for her I was in the middle of a realistic wet dream. Tiny, soft hands gripped my dick. My eyes popped open to see a real-life naked Kiara with her head in my lap. Her silk scarf was still wrapped around her head. She was face down, ass up, and if I wasn't sure I loved her, I could lay those concerns to rest.

I'd had plenty of sex in the past. I was quite familiar with lust. This wasn't that. I loved Kiara, even when I didn't know how talented she was with her mouth. I cared about her son and was committed to find out who the hell had the balls to stalk her. Moisture from the sides of her mouth dripped down the sides of my meat.

Sloppy toppy. Kiara was the freak. My reputation was historic, but this woman was nasty in real time.

"Fuck, baby." My toes curled. I gripped the back of her head and prayed she was good with it. In the past, I wouldn't give a shit if what I did was disrespectful. If I had consent, the rest was details. Kiara was my lady now—what she wanted mattered.

I tilted her head up by lifting her chin. The eye contact made the bottom of my balls tingle. If that wasn't enough to have *me* climb the walls, the sound and vibration of her hums on my dick had me ready to change my last name to Towns. She moved my hand and placed it to the back of her head. I pulled her face into me and lifted my hips to meet her mouth. *Damn, I love this girl.*

"I'm about to…" I tried to move my hand from her head, but she replaced it again. When I gazed down to appreciate Keke's work and saw her hand between her legs pleasuring herself while she gave me head, I exploded.

"Fuck!"

To add insult to a heavenly injury, she kissed my dick and licked my balls.

I pulled her up. "Enough, Keke. Shit."

She smiled at me and added, "Good morning, baby."

Before I could muster the strength to speak, her phone rang. *Saved by the bell.*

"It's Shay. She called a bunch of times last night," she said to me with concern tattooed across her talented face.

"Go ahead and answer. You've done your job and then some."

She leaned down from her upright position and laid a juicy kiss to my lips.

"Slow down. Where are you?"

I sat up and rested against the headboard. I was in shape, but apparently fucking all night and getting head from Kiara didn't have shit on my workouts.

Kiara gasped then put her friend on speaker.

"Fucking Quincy."

My eyes popped open and swung in Kiara's direction.

"They're kicking it," Keke whispered.

"Not anymore!" Shay squealed. She slammed her car door and rustled with her belongings as she walked.

"What happened, and where are you?" Keke pressed.

"I'm at the police station. I was at his house last night, and ever since you showed me his TV debut, I didn't trust him. He got up to use the bathroom, so I went through his phone."

"This fool don't have a passcode?" I muttered.

Kiara glared at me.

"You can have mine. I ain't got shit to hide, baby." *Damn, I'm pussy whipped.*

She smiled then turned her attention back to Shay.

"He does have a code, but if you get to the phone quick enough, you don't need it. Pictures of Kiara were all up and through his photos app. There were pictures of her with Kace at practice and at the grocery store. But none of them had her looking at the camera. I could scream. My hands are shaking."

Kiara and I were quiet as she continued.

"Girl, there were pictures of us at the beach and a couple of them with you and Nick together. Y'all were at an arcade. This shit looked like something from a crime miniseries. I got the hell out of there when I saw a video of the side of your house. What would possess his crazy ass to document any of this?"

She was out of breath when she finished.

Kiara shook with fear, and my damn heart rate tripled. I stood up and snatched my clothes. I was dressed in seconds.

"Where does he think you are, Shay? Are you safe?" Kiara asked as she covered herself with a robe. Her eyes never left mine.

"I left there with his phone. He was taking a shit."

The police promptly asked her questions, but I wouldn't sit idly by.

"Where are you going?" Kiara asked me with her hand over the phone.

"Coach Malcolm looked me in the eye, knowing he was trying to fuck you. He had the nerve to stalk you."

Kiara was scared, but every inch of my body was on the offense. I was ready for war. The police had one chance to get this asshole away from Kiara; after that, he would have to answer to me.

Her eyes filled with tears. "Don't leave."

Powerless. I wouldn't leave her, but that meant Coach Malcolm could roam the streets.

"Please," she added.

"You may as well head this way yourself, Key. You need a restraining order," Shay advised. "I'll keep you posted."

Kiara ended the call while I paced her room. She sat down with a far-off look on her face.

"I trusted him. I trusted that he wanted what was best for Kace."

The fire in my belly grew. He'd taken advantage of the power dynamic. If he had any game, he would've asked her out. Her whimpers broke me from my introspection. I walked around the bed to find Kiara in tears. I sat down beside her and shifted her onto my lap. "It's OK, baby. You're safe with me. I swear. I got you."

Kiara

It had been three months since Shay told Nick and me about Coach Quincy Malcolm. The eerie feeling had finally stopped now that I filed a protective order against him, and he'd been served. The police officer who couldn't keep his eyes off my ass told me he'd moved out of Saint Des since. Kace was mostly unaffected since the assistant coach had taken over during the summer league. The new coach raved about how much of a leader Kace was, and I owed those improvements to Nick and his positive influence.

Nick and I had gone on a ton of dates and had even done a few outings with Kace. Darian still didn't like that Nick was around, but he had to admit he'd seen a change in our son. Plus, his plate was full with his girlfriend who was due any day.

The lease on the home I rented was up a month ago. When I told Nick, his response was I should move in with him. I waved him off, but he was persistent. I put off renewing my lease until the last minute. I was torn between how well Kace would adjust and the fact that our home reminded me of my stalker. I relayed this to Nick who said he'd do all the heavy lifting. While I was away on a dance audition, he had my entire house packed up for me. All I had to do was decide which boxes would stay with us and which would go into storage.

To my surprise, Kace loved having Eli and Elle around, and I enjoyed Nick's sister. She was sweet, and although she was quiet, we clicked instantly. Nick spoke to the kids in a real way, letting Kace know Eli and Elle would eventually move out with their mother, but until then, we were one big, happy family.

Today, Nick and I were on the way to his parents' house. I'd met his dad briefly, and Jackie and I had grown close, but this time, I'd also meet his mother. I was about to sweat out my shirt. I was nervous.

"You'll be fine."

Easy for him to say. Nick and I spoke a lot about his family. He'd only brought home a handful of women as a teenager, mostly out of respect. I was his first relationship as far as they were concerned.

I blew out a breath and steadied myself. "Cyrus is coming, right?"

I liked Nick's fraternity brother, Cyrus. He and Nick reminded me of how Shay and I were when we were together.

"Yes. His hungry ass is never turning down my mother's offers to visit."

Nick opened my door and grabbed my hand.

"How did it go with his uncle Mitch?"

He paused dramatically. "You're looking at the newest instructor of *Fine and Fitbody Bootcamp*!"

I crossed my arms over my chest. "Don't make me fight an old lady."

He laughed and reclaimed my hand, but I was as serious as their glaucoma medicine. Nick was the kind of fine that made a person step outside of their character. These normally religious women would lose their religion once they saw a sweaty Nick Young.

We were greeted by the stunning woman from the photos at Nick's house—his mother, Brooke Young.

She welcomed me with open arms. "I was starting to believe Nick and Jackie made you up," she teased.

"No, ma'am. I'm real."

"Yeah, she is," Nick added and kissed the back of my neck. I blushed and hoped I hadn't made his mom uncomfortable. I hadn't.

Her husband, Jerry, gave me another polite nod, then asked his son, "Why are you always here? Don't you have food at your house?"

"Haha, old man. Mom invited us."

The five of us settled into the large dining area. Jackie and the kids opted to stay home to spend some quality time together without Nick and me. Cyrus who was the fifth wheel, joined us. He was unphased by the lopsided dynamic.

Nick helped his mother place serving bowls full of mouth-watering food, and after his dad blessed it, we all dug in. We made small talk and did our best to dodge questions about how we met exactly.

"Jerry told me about the incident at your house," Mrs. Young said.

I swallowed hard. I didn't want to think about it. Nick squeezed my thigh under the table to calm me.

"It was rough on her, but she's with me and Jack now," Nick said on my behalf.

"The two of you must be quite serious if you're living together."

I nodded. "Yes, ma'am. Nick has been super patient with me. I wasn't the nicest when we met."

Nick almost choked on his water. "She was downright mean."

His mother regarded me for several moments, and I hoped she still liked me after what he said.

"Good." She gave me a knowing smile.

"Mama," Nick whined.

"I didn't meet a lot of these women, but I know they let you get away with murder. Kiara sounds good for you."

I heaved a sigh of relief.

"Did you know today is Keke's birthday?" Nick added. He smirked down at me and winked.

I didn't mind celebrating my birthday, but I also wouldn't make a fuss. I was low-key about it, and Nick was aware. He was in a playful mood today and showing out in front of his folks.

"Happy Birthday, sweetheart," Mrs. Young crooned. "Do you celebrate?"

"Nothing too big. I usually go to dinner or something chill like the movies," I said, swatting Nick's hand off my thigh since he had jokes.

"And what did you get her for her birthday, Nick?" his mother pressed. I liked her. She didn't miss a beat.

Nick hopped up and ran to his car. We all sat with puzzled looks on our faces. When he returned with a small black box, my mouth fell open. I was in a real-life fairy tale.

"Open it!" Cyrus blurted.

I did. And I wouldn't lie, I was disappointed as hell to find a pair of diamond earrings. I forced a smile and leaned up to hug him.

"Thank you."

He kissed me and responded, "You're welcome, baby."

I wasn't sure what I expected. The earrings were flawless. They were obviously expensive. He'd bought them without my knowledge and presented them in front of his best friend and family. I was out of my mind to assume there would be anything more between us. Still, I couldn't shake the disappointment.

We spent the remainder of our meal engaged in small talk. When Nick's mom offered me a pecan chocolate chip pie, I fought hard not to turn up my nose. It was one of the best pies I'd ever tasted.

Jerry piped up.

"Cyrus, when are you going to get yourself a woman and stop running these streets?"

The challenge in Jerry's eye reminded me of Nick.

"Don't get these kids all riled up," Mrs. Young warned.

Cyrus narrowed his eyes. "Why are you always on my case, Mr. Young? I don't bother anybody."

"Except for the fathers of the women you ruined," he continued.

"Jerry!" Nick's mother exclaimed.

"It's OK, Mrs. Young. I've been sitting on this one for a while, but now seems like a good time to share it." Cyrus scrolled his phone and pulled up a video. It was a video from the 90s, based on the hair and clothes of the people in it.

Is that...

"Dad? Momma?" Nick screeched.

The clip was of Nick's parents grinding on each other next to an old school car. Brooke Young wore a hot asymmetric hairstyle with large gold earrings, while Jerry sported a short flattop with a tight shirt and an impressive mustache. I slapped my hand over my mouth and tried not to let the laughter slip from my mouth. The Freaknik story was true.

Cyrus laughed until Nick swatted him with the back of his hand. "Where did you get this?"

"It was online. At first, I wasn't going to show you how fine your mom was back in the day. No son should have to see this. But your pops is always on my head about something."

Jerry shrugged. "I don't see anything wrong with it. In fact, send me a copy." Jerry pulled his wife's chair next to his and whispered in her ear.

"Oh hell," Nick chirped. "We're out." He grabbed my hand, and I was grateful I'd finished my dessert since our get-together had been cut short. "You see what you did?" Nick asked Cyrus as we headed through the living room.

A knock at the front door got everyone's attention. Before we could head out, an attractive older couple the age of Nick's parents entered with warm smiles. They had to be more family.

"Shit," Nick mumbled.

"Hello, stranger," the woman said as she pulled Nick into an embrace. "Who is this beautiful young lady?"

Nick beamed and introduced me to his aunt Reese. His light-hearted mode faded when he addressed his uncle Ron.

"Were you heading out? I would love to visit with you if you have the time."

Nick was in deep thought. I smiled awkwardly because he didn't want to stay.

"How's Jackie?" his aunt whispered to him while her husband greeted his folks.

"She's doing much better. She and the kids live with me right now."

"It's a damn shame she started running wild. Looks like she never recovered," his uncle said. I didn't know how close Nick and his sister were to this uncle, but he was kind of an ass.

"What?"

Oh, no. Nick is pissed. Nick did not play about Jackie Young.

His uncle Ron turned in his direction. "Drugs. It's a shame she allowed those uppity private school girls to pressure her into drugs."

"Don't speak on my sister like you're better than her," Nick roared.

"Nick," his mother fussed.

"No, Mama. He waltzed in here and is talking about Jackie like his shit don't stank. With all due respect, Uncle Ron, don't throw stones."

His uncle puffed his chest, and Nick didn't back down.

"Baby, let's go," I tried.

He peered down at me but didn't move.

"Listen to your lady," his uncle taunted. He turned his back to us and mumbled, "Freak Nick. Boy got some nerve."

"Ron, that's enough," Brooke spat.

"Does Auntie Reese know the secret you made my baby sister keep?"

Blood drained from his uncle's face. An eerie silence hung in the air as his dad and aunt halted their conversation.

"What are you talking about, sweetie?" Nick's aunt asked him.

I placed my hand on his back. Nick was fuming, and I didn't know how to help him through this. I wanted to look away.

"I'm sorry, Auntie. Your husband should be the one to tell you."

"Ron, what is Nick talking about?" Reese asked.

Ron sat in a nearby chair with his hand covering his mouth. Whatever he'd done had him shook and Nick enraged.

"Do you remember when Jackie suddenly didn't want to be around anymore?"

His aunt shook her head, and her eyes watered.

"Nick, what the hell are you doing to my sister?" his dad boomed. She was visibly in distress, and it was because of Nick's line of questioning.

Nick kept his eyes trained on his aunt. "She didn't want to stop coming around. She loved you and was crushed when her uncle asked her not to tell you she caught him with your neighbor Tonya."

Reese squeezed her eyes shut. Brooke gasped, and Nick's father lunged at Ron. Cyrus had to restrain Jerry to get him off.

"You piece of shit. How could you?" Reese screamed. Brooke closed the distance between them and held her hand. "I knew about Tonya. I chose to overlook it. He swore that was the last time. But this… Jackie." Tears streamed her face. "In my heart, I was never settled that she wanted to put distance between us. I failed her."

"No you didn't, Auntie. He did. Jackie fell into the wrong crowd once her safe space was snatched from her, and she had to bear the weight of *his* reckless behavior," Nick responded.

Cyrus had Jerry almost in the other room when he yelled, "Get yo' ass out my house."

Ron left.

We stayed at his folks' house for another hour. His aunt called Jackie, and Nick said it was exactly what she needed. As far as their marriage, he wasn't convinced they could survive it. Brooke apologized for ruining my birthday. My concern for Nick and how he would handle what happened with his family had caused me to momentarily forget what day it was. As long as he was okay, that was all that mattered.

Nick

Kiara had an attitude. I'd complimented her mean ass on how far she'd come, but here we were again. She'd been supportive when I outed my uncle, but now that I was good, she was on this shit again. Kace was with Darian, and Jack and the kids were holed up in her room watching movies, which meant we had the freedom to enjoy ourselves without fear of interruption. Instead of taking advantage of an opportunity for me to get some cheeks before her period came, she sulked as she flipped through the channels.

Kiara and I didn't argue much. We only bumped heads when it came to Kace. As time went on, she agreed she wanted my help but was guilty of wanting to micromanage how I did it. I shut that shit down immediately, but from time to time, she would still get in moods if I allowed Kace to endure his own natural consequences.

This was different. I checked my phone because I had the pussy app to let me know when her cycle was due. I was of the mind that a period couldn't stop shit but a sentence. I only kept track to know when day one was. I let her breathe unless she came for me, then it was on.

"Are you going to talk to me? Or you going to have an attitude all night?"

She sighed. "What?"

"You heard me. What's wrong with you? Did you not have fun at my folks' place? Before everything with my grimy ass uncle."

Her eyes slid in my direction then back to the television. I moseyed to the screen and turned it off. Once I was back in front of her, I dropped to my knees to meet her eye line.

"What I do?" I laid my face on her thighs and gazed up at her. It was a surefire way to get her wet.

She huffed. "It's embarrassing."

"Impossible. Somebody as fine as you can't do anything cringey in my mind. I walk in the bathroom when you're in there. If that don't embarrass you then—"

She pushed my head and muffled her laughter.

"Spit it out, Keke." I wiggled my eyebrows. "This will be the only time I tell you to do some shit like that." I shivered, thinking about the number of times she swallowed my seed while she looked in my eyes.

"I thought you gave me a ring as my birthday gift," she said quietly.

I stood. "Is that all?" I chuckled, but she didn't find it funny. She hopped off the bed and stormed into the adjoined bathroom, slamming the door behind her.

I knocked lightly on the locked door.

"I'm not shitting, Nick. Go away."

I laughed again. "I'm not laughing at you," I tried.

"So, I'm crazy? Because you haven't stopped laughing at me." She was cute when she pouted.

"Open the door. I want to talk to your face. Please?"

She did.

I grasped her hand and pulled her to sit on the bed with me.

"I didn't want to rush, and I didn't know if you were on a permanent commitment yet. You know I want you to be Mrs. Freak Nick Young."

She swatted me, failing to hide her gorgeous fucking smile.

"I'm serious." I looked away and mumbled. "I got a ring anyway."

This violent girl pushed the back of my head. "Damn, Kiara."

"Stop playing. I said it was embarrassing."

I rummaged through my nightstand and gave her another small box.

"Nick, I love my earrings, but—"

I shifted myself to the floor and had to shake my head not to focus on how close I was to our pussy. She laughed, although her eyes filled with tears.

"I don't know shit about marriage, except what I saw my still-fucking-ass parents do. If seeing a successful marriage, plus the fact that I love you with my whole heart is an indicator of how well I'll do, we in there. I never saw myself settled down. I also never thought I had what it takes to do it, until I met your mean ass. I'm not saying we have to get married tomorrow. We can wait and date and fuck more, or we can roll up to the courthouse. All I know is you're it for me—you and our pussy.

"If you want more, maybe you can push another kid out of our glorious, magical pussy."

"Nick—"

"Excuse me, I'm proposing. All jokes aside. If you trust me to figure it out, that's all I need. Will you marry me, Girlfriend Keke?"

She knocked me down. It was like fuck this ring and this proposal because she'd tossed her robe and had her hands down my pants.

Between kisses, I asked, "Is that a yes?"

"Yes. Now will you please fuck me?"

That was all she had to say.

CHAPTER 16

Kiara

I worked my ass off to land this audition. According to the blogs, Nick called in a favor because of his public sightings with Zanaé, but that couldn't be further from the truth. For one, I was secure in our relationship. My fiancé was faithful. But I wasn't a fool. What woman in their right mind would push their partner into more communication with one of the sexiest R & B stars of all time?

I submitted applications for this like everyone else. This was a once in a lifetime opportunity. If selected, I would dance behind Zanaé in her upcoming music video to be shot in Saint Des. Nick had been escorted out of the auditorium for tussling with another dancer's boyfriend. Kace texted me that Nick and the other man had gotten into an argument about who would get the coveted spot.

My man was loyal to a fault. While he may not have fully understood the ins and outs of dancing, he was more than familiar with competition. Kace said the beef escalated, and when the girl's boyfriend got in his face, Nick choked him. I did my best to focus on the task at hand. The thought of Nick's hands around the op's neck for me had me distracted and hot.

My life had taken a complete turn for the better. This was the most unforgettable summer ever. My dreams would come true if I could only keep the contents of my lunch where they belonged. There was more than half an hour of wait time, and the other dancers and I were cooped up together. I was familiar with most of the contestants, so drama was minimal.

I closed my eyes to breathe until her shrill voice pulled me from my meditation.

"I can't wait to dust your ass."

Sierra. I'd bumped into her once since Nick and I were official, but I was with Kace. She had enough sense not to approach me then. I hadn't gotten lucky this time.

"You know her?" Michelle whispered. She was a local dancer who taught classes at Saint Des Community College. We'd collaborated on the *Ebony Moves Dance Studio* end of year presentation.

"Unfortunately."

Sierra looked amazing, as per usual. Her leotard was a second skin, and I high-key wanted to know what the meal plan was. Nevertheless, Sierra would have to claw this gig from my cold, dead hands. I liked Michelle, but even she would be a runner up to me.

"Know when you're kissing him—"

With all the good dick Nick threw my way, my inner bitch had been in hibernation. My inner B reared her head at the venom this chick let fall out of her mouth.

"Right! When *I'm* kissing him! You and the rest of my fiancé's body count were practice, and I ain't complaining."

The blood drained from her lightly toasted skin as her eyes fell to my left hand. It wasn't my intention to rub my new status in her face—it wasn't my style. But I wouldn't back down. Nick was mine, just like this audition. I stood and walked around her slowly. She didn't intimidate me one bit.

Michelle cackled, and a few of the other girls joined in. I shrugged and continued my pre-audition warmup.

"Numbers one through twenty-five," a woman with a headset yelled.

Michelle, Sierra, a group of other women, and I filed into a small classroom. We'd dance at least twice today—once here and the next in the auditorium—then if we were lucky, we'd get a callback for the job.

The choreographer showed us the routine, and once again, my stomach gurgled. She moved with precision and lightning speed. I zeroed in on her movements, using my small area to parrot her. We had ten minutes to watch and five minutes to run through it. Out of twenty-five, only ten would advance to the auditorium.

The choreographer's assistants walked the tight spaces between us, wordlessly observing. I was built for this. The more eyes on me, the more motivation to share the gift I was given. Kace and Nick may have been amazing athletes whom I mostly couldn't relate to, except when it was showtime.

The music started, and Sierra sashayed her stacked body directly in front of me. I let her have it and shifted to the left so I could still be seen from each direction. Sis was focused on the short game. What she'd done was show the production she wasn't a team player.

There was a sweet spot where most dancers lived—we did the choreography, but we made it our own. My freestyle caught the eye of the choreographer, so much so that she side-stepped Sierra to get a better view. We had the freedom to do as we wanted with the last twenty-four counts of the dance. The end of the performance was what they would remember when they made their cuts, so I slid into a split in time with the last note. It earned me an applause and an 'I see you, number seventeen,' from one of the assistants.

We were permitted to get water but not to fully catch our breath when the assistant shared the nineteen of us who wouldn't progress to the auditorium.

"We'd hoped to have at least ten in the auditorium, but Zanaé would have our heads if we sent more than the six of you who were top-tier."

I'd prayed each time I practiced that I would be blessed with the opportunity to be in the same room as Zanaé. While we were all shocked that she was in Saint Des, this was what I'd set out to do. My family, including my mother, father, stepbrothers, Shay, Jackie and her kids, and some of my students were in the auditorium for moral support. I'd purposefully invited them—and Nick's out of control self—for motivation. I would dance for the crown as if the Superbowl ring was on the line.

Michelle was one of the nineteen who'd been cut, but Sierra made it through with me.

"You have to win it for both of us," she said with a smile. Michelle was paid. She didn't need the money and probably showed up to push herself outside of her comfort zone. Along with her teaching gig, she taught private lessons to rich kids on the north side. The money was ridiculous. She could live comfortably without her community college position.

"I got it in the bag," I said with my hands still on my head. The others filed out, leaving us to mentally prepare for a once in a lifetime moment.

Nick

Kiara would kick my ass the moment she laid eyes on me. I had one job. She stayed on me about my anger now that Quincy Malcolm had left her alone. Keke would remind me if she wasn't in any real danger, to let it ride, or I'd end up in jail and unable to protect her at all.

I paced the reception area of the lobby, afraid for my life. This was an important moment. I'd seen her drag herself out of bed at the ass crack of dawn to prepare for this moment. She ate clean and stayed away from alcohol. I saw her practice routines, and although my dance IQ consisted of twerking and a two-step, it was obvious what she did was difficult.

This was the dance version of a championship game. Zanaé was Kiara's favorite artist. Today, she would get to audition for a spot in her video. I cracked my knuckles and prayed for a miracle. Kace promised to record it on his phone, but it wouldn't be the same.

"Nick."

I whipped around to see a group of people part to allow Zanaé to step forward.

"I thought that was you," she purred. Every word this woman said sounded like a song… or phone sex.

"Hey, superstar."

She leaned up for a hug then crossed her arms. "Why are you here? This audition is to replace my *female* background dancer."

"Haha. My fiancée is trying out." I ran down the altercation between the other guy and me and how my hands slipped and ended up around his neck.

"Oh, you most definitely have to get inside. Ain't no weddings getting canceled on my watch."

Her assistant kissed his teeth. "We're late. We need to get you in your chair."

"Of course. Anton, make sure Nick is left alone. Matter of fact, get him a seat beside me so his girl can see him while she dances."

The assistant—whose skin was as flawless as Zanaé's—huffed. His fingers moved double-time over the screen of his smartphone.

"Done. Can we move now?" he fussed.

Zanaé nodded. When her team moved, I was on their heels. My prayers had been answered.

Kiara

I was always nervous until the music started. The six of us filed on stage in our prospective positions. We would repeat the same routine, only this time we'd be in front of Zanaé. My stomach gurgled again. And I made the rookie mistake of looking out into the crowd. My people waved and hooted.

It wasn't until Nick's baritone rang out that I saw him seated next to Zanaé. How the hell? Hadn't he gotten himself kicked out?

"I love you, baby! You got this. You trained for this shit!" he boomed, earning him laughter from the crowd.

"OK, Nick. We know you're gone over one of the contestants. And y'all know I'm an advocate for black love, right?"

The crowd went wild. They would've cheered for anything she said, but romance was her brand.

"But I'm not playing favorites. This fiancée of yours has to earn it. That goes for the rest of you ladies. Stand out without forgetting the choreography. I want to see your personality. The more authentic you are, the better it'll translate on camera."

I nodded. I was ready. This was it. The music started, and my nerves dissolved. It was me and the dance. The only person I heard was Nick. I guess he did get my sport. I lost my footing once but recovered quickly. It happens, but the show must go on.

I gave the audition my all and left it there on the stage. I did the split again. My crazy ass man hopped out of his seat, ran up the small steps, and pulled me to my feet.

"You fucking did that shit, Keke." Nick kissed me like we were alone, and I let him. Whether I got the part or not was neither here nor there. I'd won, and no one could tell me otherwise!

Nick

Every time I watched Kiara in Zanaé's video, my dick got hard. Not only did she get the part, Zanaé let her do a little acting. Kiara had star power, and it showed. My baby was a beast. I had a class at *Fine and Fitbody Bootcamp* in an hour. I would have to delay clapping my future wife's cheeks until later.

When I looked over at Keke, who was supposed to be making wedding plans, her eyes were locked on my sweats.

"I know that look. I have to go to work," I whined.

She lifted her shirt like what I said didn't mean shit. If I was late, Uncle Mitch would kick my ass.

"Baby, don't do that. You know an hour isn't enough time."

She stepped out of her joggers and stood with her plush body facing mine. I stood, too, because fuck that job. She turned to close the blinds.

"Leave 'em open," I demanded.

"Those construction workers are still out there. They can see."

The whole neighborhood could hear them clanking. They'd terrorized the shit out of me all week with the noise. They shut down part of the street and left their tools in my yard during their two-hour lunch breaks. At any given time, three to five of them sat scrolling smartphones or peeping at my girl. They would get an eyeful today.

I stared at her. "Let them watch if they want to. It's not like they can have you."

She was braless most days. The only thing she wore was a bright pink thong. The men were less than fifty feet from my bedroom window, and the moment her ass was uncovered, their hushed conversation halted.

"Do the dance routine from the video."

The sides of her lips curled upward. Keke wasn't shy, but she used an entirely different energy when she danced. It was sultry and captivating. She twisted her arms like a belly dance, twirling her hips all the while. She bent down, and I could hear the men failing to mute their verbal excitement.

The whole scene turned me on.

I walked over to her and lifted her into the creases of my arms, then shifted her until her legs rested on my shoulders. I gripped her ass and used my nose to move the tiny fabric covering *my* pussy. Now that she had my ring on, it was mine. These fools could watch, but Kiara Towns belonged to me.

With one swipe of my tongue, Keke's body folded forward. Her bare titties rested on my head while I drew tight circles with my tongue between her legs. I'd completely forgotten we had a crowd as I feasted on my future wife. I sucked and I slurped right through her orgasm. I adjusted us—allowing her to slide down my body— and kept my grip on her hips when she attempted to move to the bed.

"Take this dick from the back, baby."

She leaned forward on wobbly legs and dropped her thong, letting me enter her while she continued to ride the waves of her aftershocks.

"You like fucking me while people watch, Keke?"

She moaned her, "Umhmm."

I slapped her ass with a moan of my own. "Fuck, baby. This pussy so wet."

For several moments, the only sound between us was the clashing of our flesh. I plowed into her like I was the star of a homemade skin flick. As long as her face didn't end up on the internet, I didn't give a fuck.

She was on tiptoes when I added, "Don't run from this dick."

"I can't help it. It's too big."

I slapped her ass cheeks again, fully aware my life would never be the same. I loved this girl and her kid. I wanted to spend the rest of my days clapping her cheeks and watching her crazy TV shows. I wanted to hype her up and show off her dancing skills, no matter how many trolls got jealous. I was in my head and in her cheeks when she pulled away.

She turned toward me, dropped down to her knees, and smirked. I would never get accustomed to Kiara's mouth on me, and she used it to her advantage. It was a treat anytime she did it because I was satisfied simply giving her oral pleasure. Getting head from her made me weak in the knees. I stole a glance out of the window then back down to her.

"Are you about to…?"

She nodded. "Who's the freak now, Nick?"

"Oh, shit!"

The End

IN REAL LIFE...

I write black love stories because I am an advocate for healthy love between black men and women. I seek to empower women to create the energy from my fictitious books in their real lives. After each of my titles, I'm going to feature real love stories. My third couple is Kim and Carl.

1. *Kim,* **how did you meet?** We met through my best friend in high school. And later reunited on a movie production called *The Gospel* in 2005. Funny story though, he had seen a photo of me that my best friend had and told her "I'm going to marry her one day" before he had even officially met me.

1. *Carl,* **what is your favorite quality about your partner?** How kind she is. And how much of a God-fearing woman she is.

1. *Kim,* **what is your pet peeve about your partner? (The thing that drives you nuts about them, but they are worth looking past it).** I hate that he doesn't share things on his mind right away, because I can tell when he has things on his mind.

1. *Carl and Kim,* **what is your advice for people currently looking for love?** -Make sure you have things in common. That way date nights would always be fun!

-Be open to try new things that will "BENEFIT" the relationship.

-No one is perfect. Weigh the pros and cons.

-Never stop being the person that your partner fell in love with.

Thank you for finishing *Freak Nick.*

If you enjoyed this story, **leave me a five-star rating and review on Amazon, and a positive review on Goodreads** and **TikTok.** And recommend it to your friends.

One of the best ways to support me as an indie author is to purchase my paperbacks. Find them on TikTok for a signed copy, or Amazon for expedited shipping.

Also, I share freebies, sneak peeks, and discounts for sensual products on my mailing and SMS list! Sign up here.

Mailing list
    Get steamy texts from your favorite book baes 💋

Thank you in advance,
    Denise Essex

ALSO BY DENISE ESSEX

More *Sweet Heat* Reads below 💋

A Justified Hall Pass

https://bit.ly/AJustifiedHallPass

Cindy Ella

My Book

Daddy's Maybe

My Book

Prison Bae

https://bit.ly/PrisonBaeTrey

The Firemen's Ball: A Masquerade Affair

My Book

The Pleasure Package

https://bit.ly/pleasurepackage

A Naughty Rendezvous

https://bit.ly/ANaughtyRendezvous

Love in the same strip club

https://bit.ly/SameStripClub

Heat Haven Heaux-Tell: Three Novellas

https://bit.ly/HeatHaven

The College Route

https://bit.ly/TheCollegeRoute

I Found Her

https://amzn.to/3VmWLm7

The Visiting Professor

https://bit.ly/TheVisitingProfessor

Gone For a Soldier

https://bit.ly/GoneForASoldier

Where to find me in these intanet streets 💋

TikTok: tiktok.com/@deniseessex222 **(Help me reach 2K 🎉)**

Amazon Author Page: https://www.amazon.com/author/denise_essex

Readers Group: https://www.face-book.com/groups/deniseessexheatseekers

Facebook page: https://www.facebook.com/DeniseEssexAuthor

INSTAGRAM: https://www.instagram.com/deniseessex222/

IG Handle: @DeniseEssex222

TikTok: @DeniseEssex222

Twitter: @DeniseEssex222

www.ingramcontent.com/pod-product-compliance
Lightning Source LLC
Chambersburg PA
CBHW071931150726
47999CB00001B/170